The Bump-Off Grind

The Bump-Off Grind

by
Franklin Stacks

Published by
Red Widow Press
A division of World Line One Press

ISBN: 978-1-945207-29-7

ONE

The woman was vibrant red. Her body flashed to each side of an orange pole. The outline of her shapely posterior teased the bricks of her club's outer wall. Bolts that held her short stage threatened to pop free from cracks and drop her to the street. She was unaware of the danger. Curved neon tubes made the dancer's body. But like many dancers who worked inside the club, time robbed her of the taut asset of youth. The line of her inner thigh flickered when she appeared on the right. Still, her rosy smile had yet to fade.

Grins widened on the mostly male customers who shuffled to the club hoping to see fully dimensional, living dancers. And drink cheap booze. Cheap coffee threatened to make Malik "Rick" Fredricks move as quickly as the red-neon dancer. Focus and relative youth allowed him to resist the pressing urge below his waist. Acting on it in the street would make him as obvious as a neon sign. Even in an age of electronic surveillance, a private investigator needed the skill of hiding in plain sight. This was especially true when your expense account only allowed cheap coffee in a sea of pricey java joints. He pushed aside urges south of the beltline made by strip clubs and fluid intake. At least while he was working.

Fredricks had arrived early to park his car and watch for Gina Tanner. He smiled as a small group of women in heavy coats deftly slipped by the horny customers collecting by the front door. The move was as practiced as onstage twirls. The women were the club's live dancers. The high-pumped high hair and tall boots gave them away. He focused on one among the pack as they moved down the alley to the back entrance. The zoom of his phone's camera revealed a young face behind an upturned coat collar. She was likely Gina under the heavy make-up and dusting of glitter. He had made his target.

Gina and her crew disappeared in the alley darkness. A blast of light from an opened door lit the dancers as they entered the unnamed club. Rick wondered if the joint was called Strippers Anonymous because no name appeared on the doors, signage, or anywhere. And there was probably no license for most of what happened inside it. Maybe the owner couldn't afford a tag and a neon dancer. The scarlet femme marked the joint well-enough. Some called it the Red Lady, or the Red Dancer. Rick called it the Grit Club because it was off the main avenue on a side street whose asphalt and sidewalks seemed to sweat. Flecks of pavement and grime slid free in the slick. The grit might foul a city street sweeper. That was probably why they never drove down here. Most of the joint's customer lit by the red neon didn't notice it. They were intent to see a different grind.

Rick leaned back in his small, economy sedan. It was an older model that burned gasoline. He could smell a hint of exhaust when he drove it. That was okay. It helped obscure the tinge of mildew from the backseats. At least nothing had punched through the vinyl. Other scents of the city in late summer flowed into his car through the space of the rolled-down window. He saw a manhole cover lit by red flashes across its sheen and grime. Underneath the lid was a deep hole. He recalled that someone, maybe his father, had said that if you ever see something punch a hole in the world, grab the edge and don't fall in. It was good advice. He wished he had listened to it.

He sighed. Technically, he still held on. He had a job, of sorts. It came after he earned a professional license on nice, beige paper. But on the job he met several people in free fall. The old tags called him a PI. The beige paper and his scratched, plastic ID listed an Investigative and Security Operator's certification, Class VI. He signed contracts to sniff out bounties for his current boss' salaried and bonded employees to nail. It was a living. Most days.

Rick rolled up his window and hit a familiar number. Acting was also an investigator's skill. He would assume two different characters for this call and the next. He'd play his first role with a respectful, assuring tone.

"Hello! Hello!" An anxious, male voice answered the Rick's call.

"Mr. Tanner, this is—"

"I saw your number. Have you found her?"

Rick glanced at the Red Dancer. He could hear music begin to pound from inside the club. The shows were starting.

"My leads paid off. I'm close, sir."

"Please, Rick, call me Burt."

"Okay, sir. Burt. I have a strong lead on your daughter—" Rick paused as an audible sigh of relief came from Burt and another, probably Gina's mom sitting cheek to cheek with Burt. Rick imagined them sitting at a small, kitchen table surrounded by collector's plates and cabinets from the late 1990s.

"I plan to contact her tomorrow." Rick continued.

"Just don't spook her, please!" A pleading female voice shouted towards the phone. Rick recognized it as Mrs. SuAnne Tanner, Gina's mom.

"Don't worry, ma'am. I'll be cautious. I'm good at my job. Even if she runs, I'll track her. I won't lose her. You two will see her again, and soon."

A set of relieved sighs buffeted Burt's phone before he spoke. "Thank you, Rick. Thank you so much. You're worth every penny."

"Thank you, sir. I'll call again with more news. And her address. You two take care." Rick clicked off before more praise came through his phone. The address he'd give Gina's parents would be the local police lock-up. That would be after his boss or one of his hired guns grabbed Diana and turned her in for the bounty on a long jumped bail. Rick was good at his job, and playing two angles for twice the pay.

"What?" a harsh voice with a slight Israeli accent shot the question like a command. Rick had hit the dial as he thought. The call connected before he was ready.

"Bibi! I have her. I'm pretty sure." Rick jerked his back straight answering Benzion 'Bibi' Rabin. Rick thought of Bibi as a relaxed dictator, but only slightly relaxed. He ran his bounty hunting business as a covert operation in enemy territory. Rick was a local asset. Rick smiled to himself while thinking of the pay Bibi would add to the fees collected from the Tanners. Then Bibi spoke again and Rick's smile flipped over.

"Who? And do you use a watch? It's late!"

"You hire me to be out late." Rick answered. "It's when your bounties come out. This one is an easy score. Gina Tanner."

"Yeah, okay. Small tag, but money is money." Bibi's tone eased at the thought of income.

"On that we agree, boss. Give another day to set this up and you can nail this chic."

"Just don't nail her yourself." Bibi's tone became almost cheerful.

"Wrong license." Rick answered and smiled again.

"You know what I mean. She's also a hooker, right?"

"Probably." Rick nodded with eyes cast to the club. "But if it's not in the expense account—"

"It's not!" Bibi shot back. "You paint this target in other ways."

"Got it, boss. I'll nail her—I mean, I'll nail her identity. Then we all get paid."

"Now you're talking." Bibi sounded happy and hung up.

Rick relaxed. Keeping an ex-Israeli commando happy was a good thing, especially when other ex-military with the firepower of a city SWAT team were his well-paid employees. Money was motivation to do quite a few more than odd jobs.

Bibi asked if Gina was a prostitute. Rick had no confirmation of such a side job. Then he looked back across the street through slightly fogged windows. He rolled his down to get a better look at the car that drove next to the club's alley. The car was too nice to be a ride-share. Rick snapped a photo as Gina's face was visible over the car's roof as she approached the car from the alley. She obviously knew the car was coming for her, but hung back as she talked to whoever requested to see her. That person spoke to Gina from the backseat. The windows were tinted. Rick couldn't get a clear shot of Gina's potential client. Finally, Gina smiled and walked around the car. The rear, driver's side door opened. Rick glimpsed another woman in the back as Gina slid in beside her.

Rick indulged in a momentary fantasy of their evening together. He just needed Gina to come back tomorrow night. Odd were that she would. She hadn't missed a night all week. Rick called his employers when he'd run up enough plausible hours. Tomorrow night he'd say goodbye to Gina Tanner. And get paid.

He started his car. Tomorrow night he would officially confirm Gina's identity and call his boss. He drove down the street flanked by seedy businesses. No. Seedy would be an upgrade. He passed some nicely polished, high-lease cars parked at what the drivers thought was a safe distance from the grit show. They parked there not for safety, but to avoid any street cameras used by the club. But they couldn't avoid the grime clinging low on the cars' paint and tires. Tomorrow they could wash their cars. The grit would roll off with the suds. Until they came back. He thought to take video of the license plates, but drove on. He really needed to lose the slick he'd brought with him in his travel mug.

Rick clicked on the radio. He still had the local Public Radio station tuned. Listening to it was a habit left over from a former girlfriend. Rick thought she was a teacher. Or maybe a nurse. He kept the station tuned because sometimes they played jazz. Rick almost liked jazz. A woman's voice related the current scandal.

"The news of the Alden financial crises deepened today when the island's—"

Rick clicked off the radio. An international money scheme would not impact him at all. It was someone else's hole. The thought of money caused him to think about his checking account and affording groceries. He recalled he needed milk and thought of a former roommate who was neither a teacher nor a nurse. Sometimes milk carton expiration dates told the guy time had passed better than the calendar he forgot to flip over. Eventually, Rick flipped over the roommate. But now Rick lived solo and in a better place. Almost better.

The next night, Rick planned to drink, just not much coffee. He parked his car a block over, and walked the street with its odd sheen to the Grit Club. He got there early to secure a good observation spot, this time inside. The greeted him from across the street. He dared to walk under her questionably secured stage and entered the bar. The smells and air were heavier in the small, dark club. The odor was an airborne cocktail of spilled booze and sweat. The sweat was from years of hustling dancers, and the anticipatory perspiration of the crammed masses of all their gawkers.

The interior looked like it was being rebuilt, but the wear and stains on the exposed beams and dust on the few, working lights showed no contractors had been inside for a decade or more. Parallel to the neon-lit bar, a long stage jutted from the back wall through crushed velvet curtains. Large screens hung bolted to the opposite wall with the same issue with gravity as the neon dancer outside. Rick figured a cable TV designer might call the style Urban Cave. Again, Rick felt as though he'd fallen down a hole. He practiced his life philosophy: when at the bottom, find the bar.

"This place got a name?" Rick asked the dark-haired, bearded and large, barrel-shaped bartender Rick thought was also the owner.

"Yeah, maybe." The bar tender answered and gave a look soliciting a drink order.

"You got a name?" Rick asked.

"Yeah. Sams"

"Sam?" Rick cocked his eyebrow at the answer while searching the bottles for a familiar label on the wall behind Sams.

"Sams." He said.

"Odd plural for a nickname." Rick replied.

"It's not. It's my last name."

"Okay. What's your first name?"

"Toms."

"Right. Okay." Rick gave up on his label search. "Sams, I'll have a Bushmills."

"Is that some kind of joke?" Sams asked. His tone was serious.

"Nope." Rick looked at Sams with a re-cock of eyebrow.

Sams shrugged. He moved fast for a big man and slammed down a shot class that had seen better days. Probably inside an evidence bag with gravel, Rick figured. Sams shot vaguely golden booze into the glass from an unmarked bottle before the sound of it hitting the chipped, polished wood passed Rick's ears. He knew it was not Bushmills. He was fairly sure it was cheap bourbon, maybe with a corn syrup chaser. He hoped it was corn syrup. He knew antifreeze also tasted sweet.

"You do good business, here?" Rick asked after his pull.

"Just who's askin'?" Sams narrowed his stare at Rick.

"The guy dumb enough to pay for another." Rick said and slapped the glass on the bar.

Sams refilled it smiling. "Yeah, we do okay."

"Better with the girls?"

Sams shrugged, but then nodded. "Boobs bring 'em in. Booze keeps 'em here. We all make a few bucks for tomorrow."

"But they don't make their money just on stage." Rick said with his best attempt at a sly smile.

"Depends on the girl." Sams poured himself a glass and gave Rick a sense of relief that the rotgut was not lethal. Or maybe Sams had just developed an immunity.

"What the gals do off stage is their business." Sams continued and downed his own shot.

"But you get a cut." Rick pushed his glass to Sams for a refill.

Sams gave a quick shrug and nod. "Keeping the stage in one piece means maintenance, and as long as there's a tomorrow, someone's gotta pay the bills."

"I guess life comes down to money." Rick said and watched his glass fill. A suspicious curl of a heavier liquid rolled inside the amber booze.

"Money. Sex. Booze. You want more than that?" Sams asked.

"A hamburger now and then." Rick answered and subverted his better judgment by downing the drink.

"Wrong bar. And do you want to stare at French fries or a French-cut thong?" Sams asked with a smile.

"If I could eat the thong." Rick looked off in thought.

"I'm sure you could, if you pay extra." Sams smiled wide and nodded.

"It would cost more than a side of French fries. Once again, it comes down to money. And here I thought love was supposed to be free." Rick gave a mock sigh.

"Love, maybe." Sams looked over at the empty stage. "Sex always has price. But, look on the bright side."

"Bright side?" Rick asked and rubbed his teeth with his tongue to check if the shots had caused sudden erosion.

"The shows, the girls, they're tax free." Sams answered. "You can't say that about a hamburger."

"Nope." Rick agreed.

Sams slid over to another customer taking a seat. The man lead a sudden wave of others packing the joint around the stage. Somehow, Sams kept the orders flowing. Rick was glad he got in and talked before the rush. Rick wondered if Sams' friendly attitude was from the fact he enjoyed seeing so many drink his odd booze as a private joke. Rick considered it the price of doing business, and maybe not the business Sams thought he wanted. Sams had guessed right that Rick wasn't a cop, but not Rick's true reason for being in the club. Otherwise, he'd have thrown him out. Rick smiled at his own inner joke.

Rick was now certain that the club's business beyond booze and the nudie floorshow meant talking to the dancers was not banned as in some, more reputable, strip joints. They did exist. Here, it might be encouraged. So long as more than talk was exchanged, via card swipe, or clean coin.

Rick was sure the camaraderie with Sams would explode once one of Bibi's men picked up Gina. For that, Rick would lure her outside. Then Sams would be down a moneymaker. Rick would lose another temporary friend, and probably need some pepto for drinking the booze. Tonight he would enjoy the show if not the drinks. With any luck, the missing daughter of Burt and Alice Tanner would be on first. Luck was with Rick. Somehow the club got dimmer. Stage lights and the screens flashed on. The music started in mid-beat. Gina Tanner, known here as Shimmer Girl, strutted onstage. Rick saw the glitter he noticed last night covered a lot more than her face. Little trails of it followed each bit of clothing as she tore them off to cheers.

Rick was certain Shimmer Girl was Gina, but appearances change with age and the wear of life's darker experiences. Rick's confidence in her identity was from high resolution, digital photos. He could confirm it for professional purposes with a comparison shot run through face recognition software. But Rick had one photo that would make him certain beyond high percents calculated by algorithms. He took a printed photo from her last boyfriend. So far, the private nudie had not ended up on a revenge porn site, but it did end up in the secure folder on his phone. He had referenced it enough before tonight.

The real Gina Tanner had a colorful, butterfly tattoo inked on her inner left hip, close to home. In the past, Gina probably thought it would be her and her lover's secret, but soon it was on display just beyond the reach of the gawking boozers as she swayed, swirled, strutted sans souci.

The recent and thankfully ended pandemic had made stuffing and tossing bills a forgotten act. Now lusting patrons threw money to the stripper by an app unfortunately called Flick they downloaded to their phones. The same phones they also used to call wives and moms on birthdays. Tonight they made Gina a bit richer for her effort. The rising dollar amount was visible on the screens to the left of the narrow stage. Hardly anyone paid attention to the screens or their numbers. Rick guessed the posted amounts spurred competition in the following dancer. Gina's amount spiked when she treated the pole as an object of climactic passion. The butterfly rubbing against the pole confirmed Gina's identity, but Rick felt no reason to rush out.

TWO

The name Cross Coast Securities read like a bank. It dealt with money, but not savings and loans. Bibi Rabin's business exchanged people for cash. No job was too small, or really too big. Some people Rick found had reputations of resisting capture with armed brutality. Bibi Rabin saw them as a market niche and hired contractors with skills more precise in the application of violence. If war broke out in the streets, and recent history nearly played that out, Bibi's Hardened Offenders Team could win. Heavily armed and relatively well paid, they redefined urban bounty hunters as a SWAT-style team never denied their target's capture.

Of course, most of the people HOT nailed were scumbags who should not be on the streets. Even ones where the asphalt seemed to sweat. Mistakes did happen, and Bibi carried heavy insurance premiums as a result. Still, business was good. Most days. The police were annoyed but the law allowed HOT's aggression inside the city and beyond. Bibi lead most of the HOT strikes himself. His stint as commando in the Israeli Defense Force earned him respect from the mostly US military team members he hired.

Cross Coast Securities was the only storefront with a locked door, cameras, and assault-rifle armed guards watching from the backroom. Otherwise, CCS appeared similar to its neighbors along the commercial stretch. Plexiglas and aluminum built most of the shops and offices. Bibi's had replaced them with bullet-resistant, transparent polycarbonate and steel.

The bright, white light tricked the brain into thinking the place smelled like bleach. It actually smelled of microwaved lunches cooked too hot in melted plastic, with a hint of gun oil. Rick walked through the few empty desks to the back. He acted with confidence among the ex-special forces contractors. At least he thought he did. As Rick entered Bibi's back office, the glare from Randolph "Rusty" Thompson did not suggested respect.

Rick had never acted on the idea, but seeing most of the men in Bibi's office made him consider taking steroids to amplify his fit but less beefy frame. The tight jacket Rusty wore seemed to be trying to jump off his well-developed frame from intimidation. Rick nodded to him, but Rusty gave no reply. And just glared. He stood by Bibi's desk while he looked at his computer screen. At least he didn't glare. Bibi was shorter than Rusty and older. His sun-weathered face and close-cropped, graying hair showed more years than his compact, muscular frame tugging his short-sleeved dress shirt.

Once, Rick once assumed the tag Rusty came from the red hair and a few obvious freckles. Bibi had corrected Rick at length and schooled him on the nickname's origin. Outside Kabul, Rusty and his unit had rescued a small band of villagers escaping an opium-cartel using them as forced labor. A band of enforcers laid in ambush for escapees and anyone helping them. As they opened fire, Rusty ordered his unit to protect and evacuate the villagers. He turned and counter-attacked the ambush. It might have been only minutes when two of Rusty's unit doubled back to rescue him or recover his body. When they found Rusty, he sat wounded beside the bodies of the ambushers. His own body was colored dark red by drying blood and caked sand. Bounty hunting, even the heavily armed variety, sounded a much easier job.

Rick expected to meet a different bounty hunter in Bibi's office. A less tense man who worked with Rick before. The missing man, Peter Berlinghetti, once held the interesting job of commanding a security squad that patrolled a section of the United State's Air Force's Nevada Test and Training Range, some of which was also known as Area 51. Pete never talked about the job, other than the tarantulas, snakes, dust, and desert heat. Pete regarded Rick with bemused but non-threatening looks. He even enjoyed a beer or two with him after a job. Rusty never seemed to work independent of HOT. Right now, he looked like a hot head. His orange-hued hair didn't cool the impression.

"This sucks!" Rusty said while looking at Rick but in answer to Bibi from their conversation before Rick came in.

"But you'll do it." Bibi said still focused on the screen.

"Pete's sick." Bibi said and finally shot a look at Rick.

Rick cocked an eyebrow. Being sick hit a greater note of concern in the post-pandemic world.

"Okay," Rick said. "Good thing he's got medical."

"Yeah, I think he's paid up." Bibi said and looked to the ceiling as he considered the fact.

"You got medical?" Rusty asked Rick, and began again before he could answer. "You got anything that will help us, tonight? Anything?"

Rick knew he could shrug and take the insult, or fight back. Verbally.

"Look, you got something better to do?" Rick asked. "I'm pretty sure this is also your job. And a job you wouldn't get if I hadn't found the girl."

Rusty shook his head in disgust but his stare never left Rick. "I can do HALO jumps, and now I have to jump on a little bitch too tough for you to handle."

"You know—" Rick began.

Bibi cut in. "You know it's a license thing, Rusty. Rick finds them. We nail them. Simple. So just shut the fuck up and just do it."

Bibi leaned back in his chair looking at Rusty. He was completely relaxed. The tension was nothing to him. Rusty took a breath and shrugged finally looking away from Rick. He seemed to relax, too. Slightly.

"I get you're over qualified," Rick said with what he hoped was a friendly tone. "But you'll like the place. Booze and boobs."

"You think I like a place like that?" Rusty shot back.

"I guess not." Rick shrugged, setting his mind for a tense car ride to the grit club.

"You guess right. Don't make anymore guesses about me." Rusty said.

"Noted," Rick sighed. "Pete and I did the lure and grab. At the club I'll make contact, draw out the target to the side alley, and you do the rest."

Rusty shrugged and gave a slight nod of agreement.

Rick gave a mock smile and walked out as he spoke. "Well, sunshine, we won't be friends, but I think it's time to get to work."

Rusty's glare returned. Bibi smiled as the two men left for the club. He knew that at least one of them would be coming back.

The red-neon dancer sign reflected off the back street's sheen as Rick pulled up. Rusty took his own ride. Rick didn't see it, but he was sure Rusty would arrive if just to follow orders. Rick assumed Rusty's ride was as armor-plated as its driver. He imagined it as an MRAP converted to electric, or a tank. Whatever it was, Rusty came up behind Rick as he came to the front door. A glance to each other was the only act of recognition. Both men pushed through the collecting customers and into the club.

The law, or the absence of laws, gave bounty hunters wide latitude for apprehending the wanted. The problem was, there needed to be a bail runner to nail. Gina Tanner was missing and nowhere to be found.

"Look, I don't know where she is." Sams answered Rick who could feel Rusty glowering right behind him.

"Yeah, but she didn't actually quit, right?" Rick asked.

"Nah. But they rarely show to say good-bye. Most of the girls just leave without so much as a flip off."

"But she could come back." Rick said. "Right?"

"I doubt it." Sams said over the clatter of glass as he piled glasses onto the bar as people packed in. "This chick is the same. She gave her roommate, Julie, her boots, so I guess she's gone-gone. Sorry."

"To where?" Rusty shot from behind Rick.

"I don't know." Sams answered. "Back home? A ditch? You can guess as well as I can. Look, I got a joint to run. But there's few for you two, just let 'em dance first. Then, private shows!"

Sams' smile sank as he looked over at Rusty.

Rick turned to Rusty, who, surprisingly, almost looked relieved.

"It's not over—" Rick started.

"It is for me." Rusty cut Rick off. "You fucked up. Good job."

Rusty pushed through the crowd. The music began. A dark-haired dancer, older and looser than Gina, did a cartwheel to cheers and began her show. Rick didn't even order a shot of cheap, possible alcohol and stared passed the stage. He found his own harsh glare and the crowd parted for him as he left.

"Yeah, well, Rusty was right this time." Bibi groaned from behind his desk.

Bibi watched Rick who sat and scanned the fast-forwarded video feed hacked from the lousy security cameras in Gina Tanner's apartment house. Rick saw a cat, a rat, and two tenants walk through the halls. No Gina.

"He's not happy. Neither am I," Bibi said. "But if you want to work here you take this next job I sent."

"I got a feeling about this." Rick said without looking up. "I saw her get in a car, a car too nice for the landscape. She was working as a hooker on the side."

"Geez! I got news for you, PI!" Bib jerked in his chair. "Hookers get into cars with johns."

"This one was a woman." Rick looked up.

"So? Johnettes? You sexist about criminals?" Bibi asked.

"No. I just think this case has—is getting interesting," Rick offered.

"Interesting doesn't pay," Bibi shot back. "You hear about the investment market? Things look dicey. I need paid bounties because I need cash in hand."

"But I think this girl was taken, not by a john." Rick tried to sound entreating, not that such a tone ever worked on his boss.

Bibi shrugged. "If so, I'm sorry for her. Maybe we'll get the job to nail the one who nailed this Gina. But until then, with no leads, you do the new job. Or I have you sign the pink slip."

"Pink slip?" Rick cocked his eyebrow. "Are they really pink?"

"Your ass is gonna be pink after I kick it. You still work here?" Bibi leaned his thick forearms on the desk and gave Rick a narrowed stare.

Rick clicked his phone and opened the folder Bibi had sent. Bibi almost nodded and turned to his screen and keyboard as Rick stood.

In his car, Rick clicked on the radio. A peeved commentator has in mid-spout off.

"—Alden! Investment there has proved a fiasco. One of the worst examples of speculation by algorithm—"

Rick clicked off the radio.

"You're back." Sams said to Rick as he sat at the bar. "You bring piss-off dude with you?"

"Nope." Rick answered.

"Friend of yours?" Sams asked and slapped a glass in front of Rick.

"Nope."

"Then—ah, never mind." Sams poured Rick a shot.

"I know you know more." Rick left the glass on the bar and practiced his Rusty inspired stare.

"So you're no cop, but maybe a PI or something."

"Yep. Right." Rick drained the shot.

"I figured that's why you always show up early. And talk a lot." Sams face balled up to his left as he made a wry smile

"Yep." Rick kept staring at Sams.

"Look, I don't know where Gina went. She was popular and got a lot of Flicks. So wherever she went, it's gotta be paying better."

"Or she's dead." Rick said, flatly.

"Nah. That doesn't happen as much as on the tube." Sams shook his head and filled Rick's glass.

"Tube? Right. So you said you've lost girls before. I'm betting some of them went where Gina is now."

"Maybe."

"Where is that?" He eased his stare and took the shot.

"I don't really know." Sams looked down and the bar and brought up a towel to wipe it. "Maybe f I did, it wouldn't be good."

"You think this is the mob?"

"It's something bigger than my strip joint. And all I want is to make rent for this place, pay the girls, and pay my own. And maybe, like you said, get a hamburger."

"With cheese," Rick offered for camaraderie.

"Never really liked cheese," Sams replied with pursed lips.

"Seriously?" Rick asked. Cheese of other varieties was this club's stock and trade. And oily surfaces were its landscape.

Sams just shrugged his round shoulders and said "yeah."

"Okay," Rick did a slow shrug. "But I'd like to find Gina. It would ease the minds of her parents. And I'm still sure you can help."

Sams nodded. And then yelled, causing Rick to jump.

"Hey, Joannie! Get out here! Someone wants to talk!"

A screech came in reply. "It's early, Sams!"

"Come out anyway, I'll lock it 'til you're done!" Sams moved to the door. Rick was glad his soul was not so callused to refuse helping, completely.

"Talk. Yeah, right." Joannie came out from around the bar dressed only in a robe and what Rick hoped was a high rise, black wig. A long ponytail flowed from it that she used as a spinning prop on stage.

"Actually, that is right." Rick said.

"Fine. I do all kinds. And it costs the same."

Rick sighed and placed some clean coin on the bar. Joannie slid from behind the bar and picked it up before saying a word. Rick half-expected her to bolt, but she smiled and sat beside him and leaned her body against the bar. Her pose couldn't be comfortable, but she didn't do it to relax. Her perfume was a clone of rosewater rolled over by the odor the air fresheners spewed in the stripper's bathroom. Her make-up was bright and heavy for the stage. And she didn't care how far her robe slipped open. Rick resisted the temptation to glance down. And then he gave in. Joannie smiled.

"Okay." Sams seems to thin, you have an idea where Gina went.

"Who?" Joannie asked.

"Glimmer Girl." Sams offered.

"I think she was called Shimmer Girl." Rick added.

Sams shrugged and went back to checking bottles under the bar.

"Right, her." Jonnie sniffed and played with the coins. "Who cares?"

"I work for people who do," Rick said. "Do you have an idea where she is?"

"Yeah, she got snatched."

Rick pitched his head to get Joannie to explain.

"There some chic, high end, she was a dancer, too. She now picks up girls for hooking. And then they go away."

"You figure the gal is recruiting."

"Yeah. Filling a stable. Guys like you come to places like this. Rich fucks make a call and get delivery."

"So Gina—Shimmer, she's on some rich boy menu."

"You got it." Joannie leaned back and closed her robe when thinking of the younger Gina. "She had an attitude. Now she's gone. Good riddance, uppity bitch!"

Rick watched the first dancer and allowed the alcohol to burn off before daring to drive. It was a lousy idea. He sat in his mildew-scented ride and watched for the car he saw Gina enter. Maybe it would come back. It was as much a lead as Joannie had given him. He'd need more to pursue the case. He'd tapped out Gina's parents and Bibi would shoot him before he paid him to seek a target on speculation alone. Bibi's gunshot would likely be less painful than crushing the Tanner's hope to find their daughter.

Rick caught sight of Jonnie leaving the club's alley. Maybe she cut her night short while still peeved at her memories of Gina who got a promotion in the hidden world of prostitution. As she walked down the street, Rick decided to go home. He didn't get there. A tall man in a dated jacket had his eyes locked on her as he followed. Rick told himself it wasn't related to Gina and what happened wasn't his business. Those thoughts crossed his mind as his hand opened his car door and he got out to follow.

He now wished Rusty was glaring behind him. The tall man closing the distance to Joannie was bigger than him. Seeing if a woman of questionable repute made it home okay might come at his physical expense. Few had accused Rick of being chivalrous. Stupid. That he heard often. Joannie noticed her dangerous admirer. She ducked into a store's alcove. Rick grunted to himself. It was a dead end.

Joannie was already trying to charm the tall man as he cornered her. Rick entered the shadowed alcove and went for the direct approach.

"Dude. Back off."

The tall man only pitched a glance at Rick over the shoulder of his jacket with dated epaulets. The style was last year's fashion and a bad retro design, then. Rick felt sorry this guy was sucker enough to buy it. Too bad for him the stretched epaulets on were annoyingly higher than his own shoulders. He reached for the equalizer in his pocket.

"Hey!" Rick barked and pulled out his stun gun.

The man turned and stepped to Rick. He halted only long enough to identify the weapon. His expression told Rick he might as well be holding a squirt gun. The guy was not intimidated. Rick knew he was now in a fight. He backed and cocked his stun gun. He hit a solid wall of epaulet jackets. Rick spun, but his stun gun was swiped from my hand. Nice and professionally, Rick noted.

"You guys all shop at the same place?" Rick asked "And I guess during the same sale."

All the men were Caucasian, tall, and crew cut. Rick sensed they were not locals. You can't tell an accent by looks, but attitude is expressed physically. The one holding Rick's stun gun was more relaxed. The others behind him seemed to hold a formation. Even the one in the alcove now stood as if awaiting orders. The leader was obvious.

"And you, guy, you get involved in things you should not." The lead epaulets said to Rick.

"It's my job."

"No. It's my job. And I don't like competition."

Rick noticed the leader holding his stun gun stressed the vowels in *competition* as he'd heard Russians and Ukrainians stress them in words such as *situ-AE-shun*.

"Then let's share," Rick said. "We aren't working for the same people. They don't need to—"

"Tonight, it's my needs." The leader cut in. "And I need you to go away. So you will."

"Okay. Just toss me my hand warmer, and—"

"You like this? Does it work?" The leader asked Rick considering the stun gun.

"Well, give it back and—"

The leader shoved the stun gun into Rick who convulsed and fell the cement.

"Hey, yes. It works." The leader said to his crew who all nodded with him.

Rick stayed conscious and slowly pulled his legs toward his torso.

"Now, you." The leader spoke to Joannie who had hid herself in deeper shadows. "You know where that girl is? The one who is now gone?"

"No!" Joannie screeched.

"You sure?" The leader asked and fired the stun gun to make it arc.

The tall man grabbed Joannie and brought her forward.

"Look! I got no reason to protect that bitch!" Joannie twisted against her captor. "If I knew where she was I'd tell you. I'd tell everything! I swear!"

The leader paused, then nodded. "Hey, you know, I believe you. Okay. Go home."

Her follower released Joannie, but a wall of high epaulets still trapped her.

"*Ungh*. That's it. All this and you just let her go?" Rick asked as he pushed himself up from the cold cement.

"Hey, shut up!" Joannie screamed down at Rick.

"Yeah, shut up." The leader laughed. "You think I'm some kind of animal?"

"I don't see a leash, so I guess not." Rick said as he looked up.

"Hey, you're a funny guy." The leader bent down to Rick. "Now, to stay funny, you run if I see you again."

The leader stood and tossed the stun gun. It hit Ricks head as they left. Joannie stepped over Rick to leave the alcove.

"You're welcome." Rick said to her as he stood.

Joannie turned and sneered, but pulled her coat and blouse open to flash him, and then resumed her walk home.

"And for that all I needed to do was get electrocuted by my own stun gun." Rick said to no one. "Such a night."

THREE

Rick sat in the dark. His apartment smelled better than his car. He still needed milk, but groceries didn't dominate his thoughts. The appearance of the fun-boy, epaulet gang threw theories about Gina Tanner into the blender. He noted their leader always used a singular pronoun even though he was in a group. That solidified his position as the man in charge. Judging from the stiff, physical demeanor of his gang with him around, they didn't just work for him. He commanded them. They weren't a collection of ex-military put together as a team like the HOT squad Bibi ran. The epaulet boys seemed to be a unit that left a military together and stayed a united. A crew of well-integrated, military trained enforcers. Mercenaries.

"Just great," Rick said aloud.

He wondered why someone needed foreign mercenaries and not just native muscle. Local thugs would be cheaper, and ultimately easier to deny. Legitimate security goons from protection firms operated out in the open. Their legal status and wealthy clients acted as shields from prosecution or too much police interference. Rick mused that the cops were controlled by the politicians who were bought by the same rich bastards buying the private security.

And then there was Bibi Rabin and his crew of well-trained and well-armed bounty hunters. He decided to be nice to Rusty, and more respectful to Bibi. He might need them. Of course, he needed an angle to hook them. Or he could just forget about the Tanner case and move on.

"Yeah, right." Rick sighed.

Gina looked across the bedroom. It was out of a fancy movie or those shows her dad watched on public television. The ones with English accents and people who stood stiff like boners. She saw the walls weren't painted blue. They were covered in some sort of fabric, as if someone glued curtains to the wall. It was all very fancy. Weird thing was the place was hidden, deep.

Gina didn't care. She already had a card given to her with a big wad tied to it in the bank. All that and so far she hadn't done a single john or shook her ass. She was told she would. There was a club connected somewhere to the hidden rooms. Maybe she was now a temp mistress for spies or something. Gina smiled. This place wasn't a ticket out of the life, but it was an upgrade. She happily kissed off dingy joints for this fuck palace. Maybe one day she'd do a prince, and then they would blow this place for another fancy bedroom with an outside view.

Gina stroked the clothes on the bed laid out for her. All of them were soft, if not her style. The skin huggers she wore weren't either. Just part of the biz. She looked over at the ornate, wooden door. It was closed, but had no lock. Still, for the money, she'd follow the rules. First, she was to strip completely, and then she could dress in the soft, frilly rags.

Her clothes peeled off and she stood naked by the bed. She looked around with a smile. Maybe someone was watching who was paying for the show. Her feet, callused from strutting in tight boots, felt the smooth carpet. She drew circles with her toes over the lush pile. Across her rear, she felt a cool breeze.

"Do you like them?"

Gina jumped. The sudden question spooked her. It came from that feminine voice with the slight accent from somewhere Gina first heard in the small limo that brought her from the strip club to these hidden, hooker digs.

"Um, yeah." Gina turned to face the speaker as her heart rate came down.

It was the woman who picked her up one night and later offered her this new gig. In the car, the woman had told Gina to call her Caroline. She was tall and made up so well Gina couldn't tell her if she was younger or older than she was. Caroline had changed from her suit. She now wore a long, tight, ebony dress. Gina noticed she had no shoes. The ones she wore in the car were the expensive ribbons of leather that held the foot to the sole hiked up by a narrow stiletto. Still, this new boss was taller than Gina. Her dark eyes didn't blink much over the delicate, European features and slight smile.

Gina's new boss stood beside a wardrobe as if she slid out of the gap between it and the blue wall. Gina noted Caroline hadn't used the door. She was the master of this strange place and knew its secrets.

"I see you've had a hard life." Caroline said looking at Gina's feet while drawing close.

"Uh, I guess. Not as bad as some."

"Well, those days are over." In one continuous move, Caroline stroked Gina's hair and then her shoulders. She knelt down and caressed Gina's feet, and then massaged their tops. Her hands moved up to Gina's calves, and up the skin of her legs.

Gina watched the top of Caroline's head slowly rise. She was confused as to how to respond, and lost herself studying Caroline's beautifully combed hair.

Caroline suppressed a shudder as Caroline's lips touched her butterfly tattoo, followed by her tongue. She felt the bed's silk comforter caress the back of her calves as Caroline's hands slid up and gently gripped her hips. Her tongue moved across the butterfly's wings along a new path. Gina kept standing as her body fluttered from nerves and pleasure.

Night could be a time of discovery. It was also a time when strange things happened, but Rick had a strange job and did strange things, so he enjoyed the dark. He didn't like being ignorant. To find Gina, he would need to flush out the mystery woman who took her. To do that, he'd need to get a bead on one or more other missing dancers that might link to this savior or abductor of lost dancers. Sams would not enjoy Rick's method to do that, if he ever noticed it.

Rick opted for an old-school form of data collection: breaking and entering. The club had a wireless network and other means to hack, but they proved fruitless for the info Rick sought. The club's employee records must be on that ancient medium called paper. That was actually smart. Otherwise, any punk could hack in and find where the object of his lust rented a room to sleep during the day. That place might even be her Ma and Pa's place where they bought the lies about her job at the vet's office going great, even with the weird night shifts and glitter.

If Rick got what he looked to steal, he could back trace former dancers. Addresses change. Phone providers do too, but the user files stick. That data linked back to a user's current phone number. And the phone user is usually where their phone is. Find its number; find the person.

Only the neon dancer noticed Rick slip by, and she wouldn't tell anyone. With the club closed, she would to continue to tease no one but rats until the automatic switch canceled her show until the dark returned. That was soon.

Rick had only a few hours of quiet to break in. The club was quiet. The city still droned on, mostly from traffic. Rick knew why he was out, but always wondered where the hell everyone else was going at 3:45 AM. Shadows worked as better protection than his stun gun. Rick's fingers slid over the two holes in his jacket the epaulet leader punched into it when he thrust the small, electric prods into his gut. Rick recovered another, more useful tool of his trade from his pocket. His Keys-All tool was loaded with more lock picks than an ego-trip level Swiss Army knife had blades. He spent more time finding the right combination of picks than popping the lock.

Rick had marked another door to the club around its back as his point of entry. It had fewer locks than the alley door, so it wasn't used much and forgotten as part of the wall. But it probably opened closer to the office. If the place had an office. Rick couldn't see wires or other evidence the place had an alarm system. But if wrong, he had a solution for that, too. He'd run.

The door creaked open with no other sounds. Rick hit pay dirt in a cardboard file drawer held together with duct tape. The same note had been scrawled on folders for both Gina Tanner and another dancer: 'bitch bugged out.' He scanned the pages with his phone's camera.

Rick smiled. *Brenda Collings,* he thought, *we need to meet.*

Rick looked skyward. Grey clouds capped the sky. Just below them were the top floors of the Gemini Towers. The buildings were centrally located in the city and close to all the tourist and convention locales. It was also the permanent—so long as the tenant could pay—home to many in unconventional professions in halls unseen by the typical, temporary guest.

These halls were not hidden, just inaccessible to the normal customer and many hotel workers. They were even a source of local, urban legends. Some rooms off these halls were the destination of the rich that enjoyed questionable relaxation practices, including carnal fulfillment, also known as prostitution.

Rick saw many of his relationships as similar to prostitution. They might have nothing to do with sex, but he still paid people for services seen by many as questionable, even legal. One such person was Harou Jones. He worked inside the up-upscale Gemini Towers.

Harou bucked the cliché of a maintenance worker as a middle-aged male with a floating gut and sinking attitude. Harou was upbeat, almost to an annoying degree. Smart. Young. His skill with aging machines got him the job he insisted be called Building Engineer. His ability to keep his mouth shut about what he saw and sometimes recorded got him decent pay, so wearing a jumpsuit with hotel logo brought him more than most who earned their pay in store-bought suits waiting for the courtroom doors to open.

Rick knew his little contributions were never the reason Harou helped him. It was the thrill to cut against those Harou considered the fat of society. Harou considered helping Rick was an act of balancing the scales. Those in suits and uniforms might debate if it was justice, or legal. Right now, Rick needed Harou to tip the scales in his favor.

Harou smiled as Rick approached him through the service entrance whose code Harou had sent him. English was only one of the languages adding to the background noise. Squeaking from the wheels on canvas bins was almost constant. They flew by loaded with laundry, cartons, and odd shapes covered with blankets. Rick heard a clanking noise whose origin he had never figured out. It was nothing Harou ever seemed concerned over, so Rick had not asked about it. Yet.

"Same fee, different place." Harou said.

"Yep," Rick nodded. "But on this one I'm going to have to owe you."

"Well!" Harou cocked his head and shot his eyebrows over his circular eyeglasses. "In that case you get the stairs, Mr. Fredricks."

"As long as I get to the right room, I'll take a catapult."

"That serious?" Harou asked.

Rick paused and considered the details that would appeal to Harou's sense of justice. "If a girl's life being threatened is serious."

"Wow. Okay, Rick. You get an elevator."

The service elevator shaft echoed with that odd clanking. But Rick was glad for the express ride to what turned out to be the fifty-third floor. He rechecked his phone locator on his own phone's screen. He had to get the room exactly right or his time was going to be even faster than the bit of hit and run harassment he planned. He entered the hallway through the elevator's hidden door. It was secured from casual visitors, but accessed by codes written by Harou Jones. The long, curving hall was painted powder blue with white molding. And scented. Rick suppressed a sneeze.

He walked to a room he hoped Brenda Collings occupied. If he was right, or rather lucky, Brenda worked for the same woman who took Gina Tanner. Rattling Brenda might cause her to phone the mystery woman. Intercepting the call would give Rick his best lead so far. Harou had told him where to find the hidden button on the door's molding that would ring the room's doorbell. A piece of duct tape from his pocket blocked the digital peephole.

He waited. Eventually, Brenda opened the door.

"Hello?" Brenda could tell from Rick's clothes that he was neither a hotel guest, a possible customer of hers, or a hotel employee.

Rick looked at Brenda and nearly fell in love. She was tall with long blonde hair shaped into a cascade of tight curls. Her makeup was a masterful blend of hues that highlighted her Nordic features. It was a masterful job of recreating a young woman as Venus.

"Right," Rick said and recovered his focus.

"Right what?" Brenda's attitude was still clicked on professional kindness mode, and she smiled.

"Yeah, hi Brenda."

"Brenda? No. I'm Vera Marie."

"Okay. Maybe now. But once you were Brenda Collings."

"If you say so. But, no. No. Now who are you?" Brenda's tone took an edge. She glanced at the front of her door and saw the duct tape that had blocked her view.

"You once danced at a club a lot of people call the Red Dancer."

Brenda's eyes flashed back to Rick. For a moment they betrayed her shock. Then she narrowed her stare.

"Brenda, I'm not looking to—"

"What so you're some old fan? I don't do that anymore!"

"No. I'm sure I would've been. But—"

"Well I don't do private shows. Not jerks who haven't been cleared medically or—I mean, shit! You don't look like you could afford a drink in the hotel bar."

"So you clear your, ah, clients."

"Of course. Look around. We aren't on the street. But maybe you should be!"

"I'm not here as a fan or pay fuck. I'm looking for a woman to save her life. And maybe yours. Who do you work for?"

"Who says I work for anyone?"

"I doubt you do the viral testing. But someone pays for that. Who?"

"You know what? Fuck off!"

Brenda attempted to slam the door but Rick caught the edge and held it open.

"I said I'm not here for that. And I am trying to save lives. You can help me. Just tell me who you—"

Brenda hurled herself against the door. Rick jerked his hand back before his fingers hit the doorframe. The door slammed closed. Brenda added more uncharacteristic noise with a shriek and killed any pretense to sophistication. Her following screamed replies easily penetrated the door into the hall.

"I got a gun!"

"Well," Rick swiped off the duct tape. "I guess you can take the girl out of the strip joint, but—"

"Fuck off!"

"My point."

Rick walked down the hall to the hidden elevator. He had done what he came to do. And she might have a gun. But she was sure to call someone, and not the cops. It was time for him to leave the scented hallway, and the hotel.

Rick was a contractor, and not an employee at Cross Coast Securities. Rick had no office privileges, not even for the awful coffee. Sometimes he wondered if Bibi spiked it extra motivators. But, knowing Bibi, it was probably cut to save money with something that looked like coffee, such as used motor oil. Rick stretched things on his own, such as use of CCS's faster and far more secure internet service. It made use of dark web search engines such as Speelurker or Blacksilk safer. For Rick.

He sat at Pete Berlinghetti's desk who leaned his butt on its left side and watched the large screen tuned to cable news. Pete sipped from a disposable cup. Rick wondered if the alleged coffee would eat through its bottom. Pete had recovered. His return gave Rick an excuse to come in the office and make use of the camaraderie, or at least tolerance, shown him by Pete.

With a name like Berlinghetti, Rick wondered where Pete's deep melanin came from on his family tree. Rick's outer bark came from an interesting arc of genetic branches. He thought of the true color of Cheddar Man, and that some modern humans carried a small percent of Neanderthal and/or Denisovan in the swirl of their double helix. Apparently, the evolutionary cousins did more than kiss. It always came down to money and sex, even when coin was a nice chunk of wholly rhino.

"Yeah, I'm pretty sure from the creak of your desk, you're not *dead* weight." Rick said as he typed.

"I said: it was a cold." Pete said, and sniffed.

Pete didn't need to turn and look at Rick to know his eyebrow cocked at the phrase.

"Yeah, a cold." Pete continued. "People still get them, despite the vaccines."

"I think you might want to say it was bad allergies. Or a headache."

As both men went quiet, the news anchor's voice became clear as an image of a remarkably blonde European woman appeared. "The financial crises linked to the tax-haven Alden grew worse when it was confirmed the head-of-state for the semi-independent Channel Island has gone missing."

"Looks like a bad time for pretty women." Rick remarked.

"You see a lot of them?" Pete asked.

"Lately, yeah."

"Lucky you."

"You'd think." Rick sighed.

"Now that one," Pete pointed at the news report just as the image of the blonde flashed to a football replay. "Her whereabouts unknown. Now that would be a bounty."

"Too bad I have no passport and Bibi doesn't cover travel expenses." Rick added.

"Speaking of—" Pete said low as Bibi walked by the desk to his private office.

"You, PI!" Bibi said without stopping or turning to Rick. "You got me a fix on that target yet?"

"I'm working on it." Rick answered.

"Work faster." Bibi said as he reached his office door.

"I could use a little—" Rick started.

"Work faster or I'll kill you." Bibi pitched a sharp glance over at Rick and then to Pete.

"I'll work faster." Rick said, and sighed.

"Gotta love his sense of humor." Pete said with a sly smile erased with a pull of coffee.

"Yeah." Rick leaned back. "I'll let you know when I see it."

FOUR

Rick hadn't worked on the new case at all. He felt compelled to stay on the Gina Tanner case, but he knew he couldn't dodge Bibi forever. Plus, he didn't want to test if Bibi could shoot him and get away with it by using some covert, commando techniques of hiding bodies. He was sure Bibi was kidding, yet didn't fully believe his own reassurance. But Rick had kicked the ant nest when he rattled Brenda. He anticipated a warning from Brenda's employer. Soon.

When the messenger came to warn him off, Rick planned to track the messenger back to their boss. He expected that boss to be Gina's abductor. Rick thought the messenger would be a wall of muscle, and armed. Maybe the person was a Russian merc. He didn't expect who actually came for him.

He sat in his car parked along the avenue close to CCS. The proximity gave him a sense of security, and the ability to sneak back in when Bibi went out for lunch. He thought about reaching for his own ham and cheese sandwich. There was a knock on his car door window. Rick reached instead for his stun gun and looked up at the person outside. Gina Tanner smiled down at him.

Rick didn't hide his shock. His wide-eyed expression made Gina laugh. Rick stared at the young woman he found and then lost at the Red Dancer. Now there she was just outside slightly curved auto-glass dolled in more subtle make-up and much nicer clothes. Actually, Rick thought, she was now wearing clothes. The designer coat hinted at an up-tick in her income. But she looked in at him with the same enticing expression she used to get gawkers to send her more money through Flick. Rick took a breath, regretted the ham-on-mildew aroma, but opened the car door.

Before dropping into Rick's car, svelte-ass first, Gina took off her coat, or rather dropped it from her shoulders just as veils were pulled to reveal sculptures of fine marble. The act attracted looks from passers-by, probably while they suppressed jealousy.

"Okay, big boy." Gina closed the door and fixed her smile on Rick as if the moving world outside had vanished. "You are in for a nice ride, and we don't have to move an inch. But I want all your inches."

"Uh, right." Rick tactfully replied.

Gina smelled as if an expensive perfume was poured into the form of a young woman, wrapped in a tight skirt, and then perched on white heels. She body alone caused Rick's curiosity to peak. The fact that Gina was now stroking his inner thigh inspired a rustle of his legs. Gina's hand hit something hard.

"Ooh, what's that?" she asked. "Your happy place suddenly getting happier?"

"No," Rick grunted. "But it would make you scream."

Rick pushed his stun gun deeper into his pocket.

The momentary break from Gina's enticing smile at close-range allowed other thoughts to rise. He considered the reaction of SuAnne and Burt Tanner if he allowed this to go on. Rick always imagined them praying for their daughter at the family's kitchen table. A candle, a cross, and a high-school photo of Gina, then a younger and innocent, served as a small altar.

"So," Rick took a breath and looked back at Gina. "Will you at least call your parents?"

"What?" Gina lurched back and looked at Rick as if suddenly seeing a madman.

"They're who I'm working for."

Gina looked off. She breathed deep, and curled her shoulders forward. "Yeah. I guess I knew that. Um, no. I won't."

"They really want you too."

"I don't have their number." Gina fired back quickly. "They moved after I left. I've never seen where they live now. It wouldn't do any good."

"They do care about—"

"Dude! Buzz kill!" Gina shouted. "I'm supposed to do you for free. That's a good deal. For you."

"Why? Did I win a prize?"

"It's to let you know I'm okay."

"And buy me off by getting me off," Rick droned. "Sounds like your new boss really cares."

"She pays better."

Rick made a mental note of the word *she*.

"I mean, check it out!" Gina took her coat and flipped up the label. "I can't even say the name on these rags."

"Nice. Look, I'm supposed to take you back to your folks. They—"

"They can go to hell! And you can—well, shit." Gina slapped her hand against her half-naked thighs. "I'm supposed to make you happy so you'll leave me alone. But, man, I didn't even know you were tailing me."

"That's the idea. So—" Rick paused and looked down the street to CCS and felt a short spike of fear. He hoped no one from there would pass them. "So why is your boss so worried about someone tailing you?"

Gina shrugged with a wave of her hands. "No idea. Look, if you don't want to fuck, maybe you can—no. Shit." Gina frowned and typically hidden furrows appeared across her forehead. "I'm supposed to Rover back."

"You pay the driver with a lay?"

Gina replied with a middle finger.

Rick considered what should be his number one option. He could stun her and haul her in to Bibi. Or he could play her as he intended to use the messenger. If he let her go, it would be as if he let a fish off the hook because he was sure it was in a bigger net. Rick realized he hated fishing. Beer on a boat deck was all right, but he preferred ribs or a burger on the beach. That, and he didn't know a soul who owned a damn boat. Gina's searching hand broke his reverie.

"You okay?" she asked. "You sure you don't want it?"

"Yeah." Rick said more to himself than to Gina who was both stroking his leg and looking to the backseat to figure out what caused the smell.

"You should go home." Rick said.

"My home, the new one. Sure." Gina grabbed her coat and opened the door. She was gone from his car faster than a fly out a window.

Rick watched her walk down the avenue and frighteningly close to the front doors of CCS across the street. She stopped and made a call. She didn't wait long. A compact Cadillac slowed and she got inside it, attracting admires whom were as relevant to Gina as the concrete of the sidewalk.

Rick smiled to himself and started his car. In normal circumstance, using a ride share gave the rider a layer of camouflage when escaping a bad date or anyone who knew their vehicle. For Rick, it made tracking the rider easier than following a car by line of sight. The three prominent ride share companies used proprietary GPS systems that had been hacked. The backdoor was a dark app that, of course, Rick had on his phone. Its screen displayed a map while a feminine voice described the turns.

A five-minute drive took twenty because of traffic, and it was light and not rush hour. Gina left her ride at the Astronomy Chateau. The odd building wedged in a corner lot was once part of a college. When it failed as a victim of a bad economy and scandals even before the pandemic, its halls and property were sold off. Its Astronomy Hall and its labs and classrooms survived as converted offices and artist studios.

The building rose up in a part of town where residents argued bitterly over whether the place was a suburb or just the edge of town still waiting for newer, taller buildings to join the aging, five-story Astronomy Chateau. Rick thought it was too bad the parts in the workshop for its telescope, the telescope itself, and dome were removed and sold years ago. The dome would've been a cool place for a bar, with or without a celestial skin show.

Rick figured rooms in the Astronomy were a safe house used by Gina's new pimp-employer. But this prostitution ring was strange. Sams played it loose at the Red Dancer, but pimps typically kept their workers in tight orbits. The trade off was physical protection, but that was usually a mask to ensure loyalty by force. It was all a subtle but certain form of enslavement. The job never came with healthcare and corporate-matched 401k.

Rick left his car and walked around Astronomy Chateau. He looked for a backdoor or side entrance. Or any low windows clear of the security cameras. The sun was beginning to set. It painted the grey sides of the building in pale orange. A block of dark blue with lighter stripes rounded the corner and headed for Rick. The security guard's uniform came complete with a peaked cap with a shiny brim. Rick suppressed a snicker at the guard's style of shirt. It appeared he had bought the shorter-sleeved shirts, but now regretted that after failing to make his arms big like the body builder on the can of lumpy, chocolate protein shakes he drank that tasted like other kinds of brown lumps.

Rick guessed they were about the same age, but different in attitude. The man's pale complexion contrasted against the blue shades of his starched shirt and pants. Rick guessed starch also kept his briefs vice-tight. That would explain why his face always fell back into a sneer. Or it was from an unwarranted sense of superiority. The later proved true.

"You!" The guard shouted at Rick although he was now within arms' reach. "You think because it's getting dark that tan of yours is going hide you?"

"Tan. Huh. I guess that's from my mom's side." Rick gave a looked over the guard with an expression of disappointment. "What did you get from your mom? Slapped around into your twenties?"

"Hey! You watch your mouth!" The guard stiffened as if he tried to tower above Rick, but they were near the same height.

"I don't typically need to."

"Oh? Why is that? You think you're some kind of tough guy?" The guard was obviously fingering a canister of mace clipped to his belt.

"No." Rick shook his head slowly and looked toward the sunset. "I don't need to because most of the people I talk to aren't assholes."

"Well I see an asshole right now, and he's in my jurisdiction!"

"Jur-is-*dick*-shun. That's a big word." Rick faced the guard. "You learn it in law school?"

"Maybe." The guard gave a mocking smile.

"Right. Because your law degree is paying your way through security guard school."

The guard flexed his shoulders and gritted his teeth. "You know how much crap I get just from being a security guard?"

"Pal, with that shitty attitude, you're going to get crap flung just for breathing."

The guard's eyes widened. He looked as if his brain was stuck between choosing shock at Rick's impudence or rage at his insults.

Rick offered help. "I think the words you're looking for are: fuck you."

"I don't use harsh language!" The guard's fingers unclipped his mace.

"You should try it." Rick said and then looked back at the sunset.

"I'm going to try something a little stronger if you don't get lost!" The guard brought up his mace and waved it before Rick.

"Look, I respect law enforcement." Rick said with a reassuring tone as he reached deep into his pocket. "But you're just a security guard. And you suck at it."

Rick thrust his stun gun into the guard's gut and he convulsed and dropped his mace before falling to the ground.

"But, like the world, you never know how bad things can get." Rick said as he watched the collapsed guard groan and twitch. "So lay there for a while and think. Besides, those blue stripes on asphalt look good. Almost as good as a healthy tan."

Rick kicked the mace into the street and left.

The sun dropped beneath the western horizon. The world grew darker. Rick resisted similar feelings in his mind. He knew letting Gina go burned both Bibi and the Tanners. He thought he could pick up Gina again. Her parents would not be very happy when they didn't find her in their kitchen but in a holding cell. They would feel betrayed. Using Gina as a way to find her upscale pimp would make Bibi mad enough to shoot him for real. But Rick knew there was more going on than a madam and her sex workers. Even if that was all Rick found, he was sure busting the sex ring would bring a slew of bounties for everyone at CCS. Even Rusty might smile. Rick thought of rolling a pair of dice, if he owned some. He just hoped his gamble wouldn't roll Gina and everyone else. Including him.

Gina felt odd. She was not used to staying put to attract attention. But that was her job, tonight. She stood and sometimes sat in the lobby of the Gemini Towers. Her feelings didn't come from the place with its over-fancy decor and looks from people passing her. She resisted flipping them off. Some of them smiled. Couples, men and women, she marked them in her mind as potential customers.

Other things made her feel odd. Caroline had given her more clothes, but these came out of her own closet and looked like they had been on hangers for a long time. Caroline also redid Gina's hair in a style identical to her own. Gina knew she was there to perform for someone, and star as a fancy clone.

As a dancer, Gina knew how to perform on a stage. She also knew what to do in a dank motel room, or the get-off closet Sams had at his club. Blacklight optional. The sign on its door read: private. The girls joked it should say *privates*, and mostly disappointing ones. She hoped never to see that room again. So maybe this act of being someone else, another Caroline, was a good thing. Whatever happened, it wouldn't be under black light.

The lobby staff had to know she was working, but didn't make eye contact. To them, she wasn't there. She drifted close to the almost hidden entrance to the hotel bar. It was dark but she could see the ornate, ebony woodwork, crystal chandeliers turned down low, and polished brass. There was no stage in sight. A large screen behind the bar played a financial news network Gina once saw on a john's phone. She could see the word Alden on a map behind the superimposed video of a blonde woman above a fancy European name.

She heard a murmur of conversation across the room. Some sets of eyes at the bar turned her way. Caroline had told her to stay free and listen. An earbud would signal her if a person who approached her was the one she was supposed to go with. No signal. Gina drifted back to the lobby couch and chairs. She had company. A tall man in a new suit not pressed after taken off the rack turned to her.

Gina heard one word. "Him."

Gina had laughed when the suited man and another one in a dated jacket put a blindfold on her. They said nothing, but at least smiled and weren't forceful. She reminded herself serial killers typically worked alone, and probably didn't own all-option Range Rovers they could afford to park in a posh hotel's garage, so she went along.

The two men were gentle enough when they guided her from the SUV into a place that sure didn't smell like the hotel lobby. That place had a hint of lavender in the air. This place smelled like a wet ashtray and carpet that saw a steam cleaner almost every half-decade.

The suited guy whipped of Gina's blindfold. Her heart sank. She stood in a motel room, or something like it. She had imagined a life of wealthy johns in posh places and maybe one day that prince would come. At least she figured she'd have the cash to buy a prince one day. There was no prince in sight. She was on her own. Gina knew the only control she had was over her fear, or at least its visible expression. She kept up the act.

The front door closed and she was alone, but a short hall connected a bathroom and another room with a closed door. A stairway led up to other rooms. The place was a townhouse. On the far wall, a laptop sat open on a TV tray. It was powered on but its screen was dark. Next to it, a fur coat and case full of cash were propped on an end table.

Gina understood they were more for show than for her payout. Circumstance, getting laid by a hooker, made them rent the townhouse. But they wanted Gina to know she was dealing with a rich person. Ego was also something she could stroke.

"Wow!" she said aloud.

"Do you like it?" a female voice with an accent tilted toward English said from the laptop.

"The cash? Yeah!"

"Oh, my sweet, everyone loves money. I meant the fur." The voice said.

"It's okay. Something died to make it." Gina shrugged.

The person speaking through the laptop paused to sigh. "All things die in time, my dear. Would you like to try it on?"

"Yeah. I guess. You want me to wear it?" Gina walked to the end table but caressed the cash.

"I want a few things from you. I want you to know I can pay you well. A lot better than what you earn, now."

"I don't know." Gina picked up a wad of bills and fanned herself. "My new pimp, I guess you still call a girl a pimp, she pays alright and looks loaded."

"I understand it's a bit difficult to impress in trappings such as these, but I assure you, my assets are better than your, yes, pimp." The voice sounded confident.

"I don't know enough to argue." Gina tossed the cash back in the case. "What do you want me to do? That guy out there in the suit? If his friend wants in, it's extra. And that's a whole lot of extra."

"Indeed it would be. I admire your courage in considering such an undertaking."

"Not that I want to, but I figure you all have me as long as you want me." Gina leaned over to the laptop and gave her enticing smile. "I doubt I could run."

"Granted. But you are not a prisoner, my sweet. Far from it. I think you'll look back on tonight and consider it a liberation."

"Okay. But I'm still getting paid. And not with a coat." Gina playfully shook a finger at the dark screen.

"Oh, yes. You'll be well compensated, sweetie. Now try the fur. You'll love it against your skin."

Gina smiled and caressed herself before stepping toward the fur.

"No, my dear. Not over those clothes." The accented voice cautioned. "First you take them off, and then you try the fur."

Gina looked over her shoulder at the laptop and smiled. She took off her jacket and let's it slide down her body to the floor.

"You know, before this week, I'd never done it with a girl." Gina said and began to sway. "Now, it'll be two before Friday. Virtual and real."

"Take off your clothes, and we shall see."

"You want me do a strip?" Gina lifted her skirt up her thighs but then let it drop.

"However they come off is up to you, but I want them gone, soon."

"Okay. You're the boss." Gina ran her hands up her body.

"My title is a touch more sophisticated than that. And more than the woman you work for."

"That's one up on me, because I don't know her real name I'm sure." Gina said with a breathy voice as she slid her fingers across her hips and up over her breasts

"So long as she doesn't know who I am, that's the key."

"Well, cool, because I don't. But I guess you're gonna get to know me." Gina twerked at the laptop. She swayed and grabbed the clinging dress she didn't like much. She pulled it to her sides. It tore open to reveal her breasts. Gina pulled it down as it ripped. She turned her rear to the laptop and bent over as it slid over her taught glutes. She froze.

The door at the end of the short hall creaked as it opened. The same female voice came from both the room and the laptop.

"Oh, yes sweetie. Oh, yes."

FIVE

Rick looked at the monitor. He used his own laptop at home to avoid Bibi and avoid his boss tracking his searches. He still hadn't opened the case that Bibi assigned him. Gina Tanner was doing all right, if you forgot her line of work. But the world she had dropped into was cockeyed, and not because it was criminal. Rick needed proof. His only lead was the Astronomy Chateau. He looked over its tenants on screen, and made a note of potential marks. He studied the building's history, odd floor plans, and its sole owner. It was possible the owner had no clue that at least one prostitute had access to his building. But people always knew more than they let on. Especially when money was involved. And sex.

Web pages, light and dark varieties, only offered so much information. Rick went on a drive.

On the sidewalk, the Astronomy appeared to follow the right angles of the street and avenue. But that was just the outward facing corner. The building's section of land was a pie shape, slightly yanked on one side. The building and its interior took odd angles to match. It was an efficient use of space. But the results, especially the side stairways, suggested M.C. Escher was the architect. Rick found himself on the same floor he thought he'd just left. Eventually, he made his way through the whole building. It was an uninterrupted recon. He learned from the tenant he conned to let him in that the security guard was out on sick leave.

Unlike the much larger and posher Gemini Towers, the Astronomy definitely had only one set of elevators that served all floors. Wherever Gina went on the inside, it was a hidden space. That would be easy enough to conceal when people expected all rooms to be shaped like boxes, but this building had walls with many angles. Rick needed to return at another time with less light and fewer occupants.

A massive, perhaps tragic complication would change that plan, and Rick's life.

'Sympathy for the Devil.' It was a Rolling Stones tune recorded before Rick's parents had been born. But once Rick heard it, he identified with its caution to use well-learned verbal tactics, or politics, when dealing with those who could lay your world to waste. And maybe your soul. But many people Rick met might not have one, or they had dropped it off the curb where a truck tire crushed it before a street sweeper spun it into its guts along with the cigarette butts, vape pens, smoked virtue, and grime.

The song came to mind when Rick entered the Southwest Police Precinct. A detective Rick had dealt with before, and almost amicably, had called him in. Rick's choice was to come in voluntarily or have uniforms bring him in, quote, kicking and screaming. Rick didn't intend on kicking or screaming, but if he pissed off the detectives, they might tell the uniforms to make sure he did. Being shocked by his own stun gun by mercenaries was enough of a bitch for one week.

Rick said he'd come in smiling. The detective hung up. Rick assumed he wasn't smiling. Rick had no idea why they called him in. He left his stun gun in the car to pass through security. It left a spot for his soul to stay tucked in his pocket.

The precinct's interior resisted the twenty-first century. It was an example of government-bought splendor when it opened, last century. The phone screens that held the attention of most people in uniforms, suits, and street clothes lit their faces in bright colors that contrasted against the building hues. Most of the original doorframes were brown from wood or just age. The walls were probably white when last painted. City air and sticky fingers had changed the hue to what might be kindly dubbed urban beige. A checkered pattern was still visible on the floor. Rick guessed its last polish was in 1968. Dome lamps gave dim light near yellow in color and near useless for illumination.

Rick almost felt at home.

Det. Whilton waited in his crammed, corner office. His and other detectives' *offices* were inside one, actual office that had been taken and divided into smaller, walled sections for desks as a cruel joke on those forced to sit behind them.

The detective was cast from the over-used and cracking Caucasian cop mold. He was slightly beyond middle age with a center of rounded mass that threatened his slacks and belts a little more each day as he worked toward elusive and probably unaffordable retirement. Whilton yelled into his phone. Of course, it was an old, landline model with a handset attached by a curled wire. Whilton hung up with like a judge slamming a gavel. Rick sat down and waited for his sentence.

"You're a piece of work, Ricky."

"I'll take piece of *work* for you, Whilton."

"Funny guy. Are you also a killer?" Whilton nodded as if to confirm the truth behind his question.

"Killer? Uh—" Rick considered his assault on the security guard and a few others in his recent past. He wondered if one of them had gone bad at the ER and now a formal charge for them or loved ones was somewhere on the morass of paper on Whilton's desk.

"No," Rick finished.

"You sure? I think maybe you are?"

Rick didn't suppress his look of shock. But quickly relaxed his face. Just as Rick needed to build a case with evidence and either give it Bibi, a client, or even the police, Whilton was doing the same. Whatever he had on Rick wasn't enough to file charges or get the district attorney excited. So he brought Rick in to rattle him into verbal evidence or doing something scared after he left. Rick suppressed his growing sense of dread, and knew he could work Whilton for information just as Whilton was trying to work him.

"Yeah, me too, Ricko." Detective Hardin, Whilton's partner and possibly lost twin parked himself at the door and gave a knowing look at Rick mingled with disgusted. "You're a real piece of—"

"That jokes has been said, Hardin." Rick cut in.

"It's not a joke, is it?" Hardin said as his face when into a look of full disgust. "Right? Ricky. Or maybe Dicky."

"Right, *Hardin*." Rick said relaxing in the creaking, metal chair. "Not like you can make a joke w/ that name."

Hardin glared. Whilton also stared at Rick, waiting for a jab at his name, too. Rick resisted. He could imagine that since the detectives became partners, the amount of jokes about their seemingly opposed surnames was, and probably continued to be, vast. Perhaps they could stand to remain partners because the jibes weren't constant. Maybe they came in a cycle. A sort of rise and fall event.

Whilton nodded to himself and then looked up at Hardin. "The death penalty. I miss it."

Whilton said looking at Hardin.

"Yeah, me too." Hardin agreed.

The detectives acted as if Rick had vanished. The subject was grim, but the detectives feigned cavalier attitudes. Rick knew it was a practiced interrogation routine, but felt instead as if he was now watching an amateur comedy duo competing at a county fair.

"I mean, we can still shoot people." Hardin continued.

"Self-defense!" Whilton said. "I mean, a popsicle stick in the wrong hands can be lethal."

"And you gotta go home."

"So yeah, that's one way of getting it done." Whilton said with the same nod of personal agreement. "But I miss that strapped down moment when the punk knew there was nowhere to run and he had to face what he'd done."

"It was beautiful. In a way." Hardin added.

"Yeah. In a way. It serves the punks right." Whilton raised his voice on cue and both detectives turned and glared at Rick. "Especially those who kill young girls!"

Rick was now truly confused. He knew they meant him as the killer, but who did the think he killed?

"What the fuck?" Rick said low.

"Gina Tanner!" Whilton shouted.

"You killed her!" Hardin jumped in.

Rick shook his head, and then found his voice. "You guys are sick!"

Whilton's round mass found speed. He bolted from his chair and grabbed a folder. He slammed down printed photos from it in succession in front of Rick. The first few were grainy shots of the two of them together. Whilton yelled his accusation as he slapped down the last few, ending with a photo of Gina's body on a morgue slab with her butterfly tattoo circled.

"You knew her! You killed her!"

Rick looked at the photos but his thoughts went to Gina, and then her parents. If she was dead, he might have stopped it if he hadn't used her to find her pimp. His heart didn't sink, it fell through a deep hole with no traction at the sides.

"You were positively IDed as being around her work place."

"Yeah, work. Right." Hardin sneered.

Rick began to focus passed his shock and anguish. "How did someone ID me?"

Whilton stayed quiet, but Hardin answered.

"They picked out your photo."

"You put me in some photo line-up?" Rick asked. "That's incriminating."

"Not quite. It's a suspicious persons' portfolio." Hardin said.

"Is that legal?" Rick asked.

"Are you serious?" Whilton jumped in. "You work for bounty hunters!"

"Well, that is legal, detective."

"So sue us!" Hardin barked. "And while you're at it. Tell your lawyer you need bail and a clean set of boxers for the night.

"Maybe a teddy bear."

"I'm being arrested?" Rick leaned back from his accusers.

"Maybe not." Whilton answered.

"Yet." Hardin added. "But answer the questions."

"Then ask them." Rick growled.

"Look, wise ass, why were you after this girl?" Hardin asked.

"Like you just said. It's my job."

"Usually the perp doesn't end up dead." Whilton fired at Rick. "Even with your boss' crew knocking down doors."

"And walls. They blew up a car last time, right?" Hardin asked Whilton.

"Yeah, but it was a compact." Rick answered. He felt more confident that if he didn't incriminate himself, he could walk out, free. "And electric. Smaller bang."

"You're gonna get banged, in lock-up!" Hardin spouted and jabbed the photos with his finger. "This kid was from a good family—"

"I know!" Rick cut in. "I know them. They wanted me to find her, too."

"But you didn't." Whilton said "Instead—"

"No, I didn't." Rick's voice found a low, dreadful tone. "We were going to pick her up before she disappeared."

"Disappeared." Whilton said.

The detective flattened the world as he spoke to avoid it sounding like a question, but Rick knew it was. The room became quiet except for the background noise of the precinct. Rick knew this was new information to them. Rick recalled that Whilton had said 'work place,' not former work place. The detectives thought Gina was still working at the Red Dancer.

The looks between Hardin and Whilton were a silent joust to see who took the lead after Rick's revelation. Rick got tired of waiting for them to speak.

"You guys need a group Heimlich maneuver? Looks like you both just choked."

"Shut up!" Whilton spat. "When did she disappear?"

"I think you know."

"You tell us!" Hardin demanded. "Explain the photos!"

Rick looked over at the photos. "I'm the PI. She was the hooker." Rick said. "What else?"

"Choke yourself, you little shit!" Hardin shouted.

Rick looked at the photos and had questions of his own. The photos had been printed from a video feed, probably a security camera. The cops could have subpoenaed the video, but why would they? There was no reason the police would be interested in Gina or him until now. Unless he and Gina were witnessed during a bigger investigation. Rick doubted that. Calling him would risk exposing that. The detectives were only interested in Gina's death. Whoever sent the video was attempting to frame him, or at least get the cops to shake him up and maybe make him back off. Gina was sent to placate him. Now, probably that same person wanted to frame him.

But did they kill Gina to do that? Why not just kill him? Gina might have died for a reason other than getting him nailed.

"Looks like you two were cozy. Why didn't you take her down right then?" Whilton asked.

"I investigate. I don't detain." Rick answered. "If she knew I worked for bounty hunters, she would have run. So, yeah, I was nice to her.

"You fuck her?" Hardin asked with a knowing nod.

"No."

"Just a blow, then." Hardin added.

"Look, I lost her once." Rick said through his teeth, and readied a set of lies. "I got my ass kicked. I found her again. Today I was going to call in Bibi's guys, but—" Rick paused. "She's dead."

"She was murdered." Hardin hovered next to Rick.

"Too young," Rick breathed. "Once, if you were young, no one thought you could die. That seems a long time ago."

"It was yesterday." Whilton said and looked off into space.

"Sorry for your loss." Rick spoke in a tone of sincerity. He didn't know if Whilton had lost anyone in the pandemic, but if he did, Rick hoped his seeming act of kindness would slow him down and his partner would assert himself. Rick hoped that would create conflict.

"Loss. Right." Hardin stepped in. "I bet you get paid anyway."

"No." Rick took a breath. "I work contracts. This one—"

Rick's genuine disappointment and grief halted his speech.

"A gig PI. That's nuts." Hardin sneered at Rick.

"Typically, it's a paycheck." Rick said.

"Without benefits, right? Seems risky." Hardin continued.

"So's your job." Rick shrugged.

"We got medical. And guns." Hardin gave an arrogant smile.

"Nice." Rick answered with a mocking nod. "I bet I get better coffee."

"Go get some. Somewhere else." Whilton said with a stern tone of rebuke.

Rick suppressed taking a deep breath of relief.

"Yeah," Hardin's face lit up at the idea of coffee. "And bring us—"

Hardin began, but a harsh glare from Whilton cut him off. Hardin's mouth was frozen half open. His unthinking request broke the edge of Whilton's harsh dismissal of Rick. He said nothing, but smiled as he squeezed passed Hardin and left the detectives in their glare versus dropped jaw moment.

Beneath the grin, Rick felt sick but felt he needed to find out more about this female pimp and her operation, now maybe to save himself as well as avenging Gina. If he was responsible for her death in some way, he would nail the actual killer. He had a crew of heavily armed actors to bring in if the cops didn't have enough to act. It was just take more evidence, or clever lies.

Rick made his way to his car in a lot that charged too much with an attendant who looked scraped from the floor of the pay booth. The idea of heavily armed actors came to Rick again, but not in a good way. Not far from the precinct, a wall of dated jackets with epaulets intercepted him.

"So I said if you see me you should run." The leader said. The same man who had dropped Rick with his own stun gun.

"I'm not Abraham and you're no angel." Rick said. Songs from the 1960s were on his mind. "Besides, I'm pretty sure I have no kid to sacrifice."

"Biblical reference. Or maybe Dylan. Odd from you." The leader replied.

"Why?" Rick put his hands in his pockets as he shrugged.

"You must think I have no judgment of character." The leader said.

"I'll take that as an insult." Rick replied.

Slowly but surely the leader's crew moved around the sidewalk. Rick knew they were not just ambling about. They were moving to flank and surround him. He figured they were edging him closer to a dark van that was double parked a few car lengths away. Maybe finding Rick was a surprise, or they had all really needed to pee. Otherwise, someone would already be in the van and driving it to him rather than the mercs trying to subtlety push him towards it on a busy street near a cop house.

Rick admired their audacity or courage to attempt an abduction near a police precinct in daylight. Maybe they had a complete lack of respect for the cops moving in and out of the precinct within eyesight. Rick needed those cops to be in earshot. He reached deeper into his pocket, but not for his stun gun or soul. He grabbed another tool that he found came in handy against thugs in crowded places. Before he used it, he kept his cool and decided to learn what he could from the enforcers for persons unknown, who might be killers.

"Hey, you take it as you like." The leader continued. "But you should take off—out of town. I don't like people pushing in on my business."

"I have no idea what your business is. But I'd guess between you, me, and the goon show, that I'm the only one who pays local taxes. Right, *Vladmir*?"

"Again, you with the mouth." The leader shook his head in mock disgust. "You think we are just uncouth toughs passing through. Like some, uh—?"

"Biker gang?" Rick offered.

"Hey, yeah. That works."

"I don't think you guys ride hogs, but I bet you guys are killers." Rick looked across the group.

"Please. We're a, ah, a moving company." The leader smiled.

"Yep." Rick slowly stepped backwards as some mercenaries moved forward. "For sure."

"And you should move out of town. Fast."

"On the next *avtobus*, right?"

"Might be a good idea." The tallest one said with a much stronger accent.

Rick smiled. He loved online translation. It gave words, phrases, and pronunciations for almost any language, including Russian. The tall one understood the word for bus. His unthinking reply earned him a cutting look from his boss.

Problem was, it also killed the conversation but not the moves to trap Rick. He pulled his little something for defense. The Russians reached for their own weapons, but not before the noise of Rick's the air horn called attention to him and from pedestrians and police.

"The *avtovokzal* is down a few blocks." Rick said while backing away. "Happy trails, *tovarishchi*."

Rick turned and walked down the crowded street in a cool and calm manner, but with as much speed as a cool and calm stride allowed.

SIX

Rick drank actual Bushmills. It was from his own bottle in his own apartment. For once, he had the lights on. Rick sat as his own table in the quarter kitchen at a table not much bigger than a toilet seat. At least the chair was more comfortable than the one in Whilton's joke office. He considered the Tanner case and how Russian mercenaries, a woman pimp, and a running girl with a sad fate tied together.

Rick figured the Russians didn't want him for information. They just wanted him gone. That meant they wanted to keep something hidden, or they wanted get rid of competition while they tried to find something. Rick didn't think they were working on spec. Someone had hired them and paid for their plane tickets. Renting mercenaries meant connections beyond most urban crime syndicates. If this was criminal, it was on a scale bigger than a prostitution ring for rich folk.

But if a scammer didn't hire guns to get their way, they might hire high-end hookers to get people to do what you wanted. In one of the hardcover books Rick had actually read, it described an ancient story of sex and violence. It might have been a pulp novel for its day, but it was the great Epic of Gilgamesh. Long before a messiah became a swear phrase, Gilgamesh used sex to quell a powerful rival. Gilgamesh sent out a prostitute to bring in the wild Enkidu. Of course, sex gave the prostitute power over Enkidu and thus power in town. This led to the dust up between Enkidu and Gilgamesh that trashed a city. Did Gina's madam fight to control something? Maybe dust was being kicked up and Gina became caught in the storm.

No matter the Russian motivation, Rick needed more info on them. Bibi might be able to give him at least a hint. But Rick needed a way to ask him that would also appeal to Bibi's profit motive. And because Rick didn't have jack for that, he needed a good lie. Rick thought of the new target Bibi had assigned him. Suddenly, a Mr. Antoine Everson had a connection to Russian mercenaries that would be as much a surprise to him as it was going to be to Bibi.

Rick took another shot, and made they call.

"Bibi? Rick, here."

"Wow!" Bibi's voice came through the speaker loud, clear, and annoyed. "I didn't need to be a PI to read the phone number. You have a place to nail Everson?"

"I got news on this guy. He's in deep on something big. I'm getting dogged my Russian mercs."

"What? Are you at a bar?" Bibi challenged. "You're obviously drunk."

"I'm telling you, Bibi, this guy is deep in something. There's a crew warning me off about him. Today they tried to snatch me off the street. By a cop station!"

"You'd better damn well be serious about this!" Bibi shouted.

"I am. So you need to tell me more. I need to know how deep the shit is you expect me to wade through to nail this guy."

"He's just some piece of lowlife shit!" Bibi yelled and finished with a growl.

"Maybe. But what he's in the deep end of the cesspool. What crews have moved into town? Are they mobbed up?" Rick asked, mixing his true concerns into his lies.

"No. I mean—I doubt it."

Rick knew Bibi's confusion was the hook he needed.

"Can you ask call some of your contacts to—"

"Yeah-yeah." Bibi cut in. "I'll make some calls."

"Thanks. I'll stay clear of borsht until you call me."

Bibi hung up. Rick smiled, and poured another shot.

Later, Rick went out to beat the crowds. He went back to the joint he'd dubbed the Grit Club but that most called the

Red Dancer. Rick also thought of it as the Non-Bushmills Bar. Name or not, he might get some info there. In part, he went to see the reaction of Sams and whoever else was around, such as Joannie, or any rats bold enough to dare the light. They might be the ones who IDed him in the video, or Whilton and Hardin might've lied. Lately, the truth was as pure as Sams' booze, if cut with rock salt.

"You're back." Sams said as Rick took what had become his stool.

"I bet you say that to all the guys."

"Mostly, I say get lost." Sams said and slapped a glass in front of Rick.

"But not to me." Rick fingered the glass. It was a good sign.

"No. No need. Plus, you actually pay. For at least half of your drinks."

"It's my sense of ethics." Rick shrugged.

"Whatever motivates your cash my way." Sams said reaching under the bar for a bottle.

"Then hit me with a Bushmills."

"Right." Sams clinked the glass with the neck of an unmarked bottle and poured.

Rick covertly eyed the glass to make sure it hadn't just chipped, and then drank. Of course, it wasn't Bushmills. At least the booze was a little more golden this time, and less sweet. Rick figured Sams was giving him the equivalent of his good stuff. He also figured Whilton and Hardin had lied. Rick's phone rang. He looked at it with some anticipation and dread. It was Bibi.

"Hello, boss. What's the word?"

"I got nothing for you, Rick." Bibi sounded truly disappointed. "If there is a merc team in town, they came in with good cover. And I can't find anyone to tell me when a crew was hired that fits your bill. So, sorry. No luck. But if these guys approach you again, call us. You're a shithead, but not a bad PI."

"Gosh, thanks." Rick said not took a shot. "Nice to know my life has value."

"Shut the fuck up, but call if you have to." Bibi said.

"Got it." Rick hung up. He looked at Sams. The guy who gave loose cover for hookers might know something about the biz beyond his walls. Things about hotels, motels, cracks in alleys. He might even know of a place that didn't stink of the sweat and multiple johns' cologne. Rick had stared at Sams long enough to make him nervous. Finally, he asked his question.

"So, Sams. Where would people might stay who have some standards, but still want to keep their presence on the down low."

"The what?" Sams asked.

"To stay hidden." Rick answered.

"For a night?" Sams asked and poured.

"For however long they want."

"Okay. Uh, the Four Winds. But they don't have a bar."

Rick thought to himself that the mercs probably didn't drink much. Or at least bought their own vodka.

The Four Winds was a bit of a drive. The row of rentals was not an off-highway Holiday Inn, but a line of townhomes. The occupants rotated through faster than most cheap rentals. But if you could pay, you could stay. The duration was by choice. The place had no leases to keep you. And if you were clever about how you paid, there was no paperwork or traceable transactions to reveal you were or had been a guest.

Rick looked over the place from across the street. He was sure the upstairs views were nice, if you liked industrial waterfront. But who wouldn't trade an ocean view for massive cranes and shipping containers? Not that most occupants cared. The curtains on each unit stayed drawn even in the day.

Rick kept his phone in hand with speed dial for Bibi's direct line. Rick was not supposed to have Bibi's direct line. But there were many things Rick shouldn't have or do. Solo recon on military trained ass-kickers was on the list. He noted there was no dark van. He saw no epaulet wearing men of unusual size. If they did rent a place there, they might be out. For their sake, he hoped they were buying new jackets.

So far, the Four Winds was a bust. But it was the best place such a crew would stay. Rick logged the route in his phone's GPS. He'd be back.

Rick knew where he could find one person involved with the case. Brenda, or Vera Marie, still did business at the Gemini Towers. She was also probably working for the madam who took Gina who probably knew about her murder.

If Rick could not find the madam through Brenda, he could find one of Brenda's clients by watching her. And that man or woman would have some form of contact information about the madam. To get to her might be fewer than six degrees of separation. And of Rick had to separate people from their dignity, or arms from shoulders, he was now quite willing to do that.

Rick only needed Harou Jones' cameras to flag a client of Brenda's that came out of her room, and then what ride he took out of the garage. Those two data points connected Anthony Oliver Cord, e-funds financier. He ran a sort of hedge fund through crowd funding. In truth, it was a legal pump and skim operation. As long as people put money in the project pool, he could take a percent of the gathered principle, not the potential and over-hyped payout.

Rick was sorry he hadn't thought of it himself. But he was about to cut in on the scam in a more direct way than writing in all caps in the comments stream. Cord's real name was Thad Bunter, but Rick didn't care. Rick just needed an address. The newly minted Mr. Cord was smart on e-money scams, but dumb enough to use a limo from a hacked ride share.

His money was piling up, but his class of millionaire was still low enough that his snob palace was in the city and near the street with automated security systems whose manuals were readable online. Rick wondered if that last part was irony.

And for tonight, the fewer human eyes that saw him, the better. No guards saw him kiss Brenda goodnight. Cameras gave him a false sense of security. But not all of them spied for him.

Rick watched Cord walk through his dark, sprawling house. He thought Cord was too young for his build to suggest the 'phrase rolling in dough' meant a lump of uncooked bread and not a pile of cash. But he had more money for beer and pizza than Rick did, and he looked it.

Cord used the light streaming in from the moon and streetlamps to guide his path and failed to notice the blinking LEDs warning of sabotage to his security system. Rick wondered if he was even familiar with it. Maybe Cord thought someone else took care of it, just as Brenda took care of his other needs. When you pay people for almost every function in life, are you a man in control or a man in need? Does the money make you strong, or ultimately weak? Rick still would've liked more money for beer and pizza. Actually, he enjoyed bourbon and lasagna even more.

Cord had no such thoughts. His memories of recent bliss flashed away when he turned on his bedroom lights. He caught a brief glimpse of the stranger in the mirror and felt a sudden spike in fear. The lights went off. Someone else was in control.

Cord made a slight, guttural sound then croaked out a sentence. "You here for her? Make sure I behaved myself?"

Rick stood on the other side of the room, hidden in shadow. He expected Cord to beg and bribe him, but not say anything like that. He played along to see where it went.

"And did you?"

"Drop dead!" Cord said but his voice suggested more fear than braggadocio.

"That might be your job tonight."

Those words made Cord pause and quiver. He mustered a stuttered reply. "This—this is my house!"

"So? Does that mean anything, now?"

"It means I'm rich." With the thought of money, Cord summoned some guts beyond the ones from good living. He turned from looking at the shadowed man in the mirror and looked at him across the room. "Name your price. You can work for me on the side. Just tell Caroline I did fine."

"And being a good boy gets you a gold star."

"It had better!" Cord took a breath. "I'm tired of being on probation. I did one bad thing on one night."

"And were punished."

"Punished? I guess. This probation sucks. Not being seen there is making people ask what's up."

Rick thought, *being seen where?*

"You sound pissed off, Mr. Cord."

"I am. Maybe not in your world, but for mine reputation is everything." Cord shook his head and looked off at the floor as if feeling embarrassed.

"Even among hookers." Rick said, trying to goad Cord.

"No. Fuck them! I mean among their customers, my colleagues. If you can pay for Golden Horizons, you go to the there. It shows you can afford it. You see the shows. The sex is a bonus."

"Right. And the other rich horndogs look down on anyone else not, well, not golden."

"Look, tell Caroline I'm under control." Cord's voice had a pleading tone. "She shouldn't ban me anymore. And she can get to me with you. I get it. But I'm under control. Tell her. So will Vera."

"I'm sure she will, but I won't."

Cord's mouth opened but he said nothing. Confusion stole his words. Then the solution of money came to him again. "Look I said I'd pay you! Better!"

"You will. But I also want information." Rick said and stepped forward but still stayed in darkness.

"What?" Cord's voice reached a chirping height.

"Caroline runs the line of women Bren—ah, Vera works with. Who else uses them?"

Cord was confused but began to realize the stranger might not be there for Caroline. "Look—! Wait, who do you work for?"

"I freelance. Now tell me who else likes Vera."

"You got some blackmail side job? Get out! Just get out!" Cord had a moment of bravado and stepped closer to Rick, but took a step back when Rick didn't move.

"Cord, you say you own this place, but you're wrong. Right now I do. And I own you. So if you don't want me doing the painful opposite to you of what little, sweet Vera does, then you'll tell me what I want. Then you'll be able to make your meetings tomorrow and I'll be just a bad memory you don't tell anyone about."

"I can't. I mean, you might beat me to shit, but any names I give you could make life and business hard for, for forever. So go ahead. Let's get this done with."

"Okay. But you're still going to tell me. It's just going to be while watching yourself bleed with the taste of blood in your mouth." Rick took out his stun gun and made it arc.

"Alright! Clayton Haines!" Cord screamed and waved his hands. "He owns the place where the Golden Horizon is hidden. You can get anything from him. Any info. Anything you want!"

"Okay. Good." Rick put away his stun gun. "Now, about my confidentiality fees."

"Fee?"

"Fees. Plural. I assume you have more than a little cash stuffed someplace other than your ass."

Rick knew it was always too early or too late to go to a bar, especially one with strippers before they take the stage or after they quit dancing. He went back to the Red Dancer, anyway. He hoped to catch Sams before the doors opened. He wondered if Sams knew about a place called the Golden Horizon, and had questions about other missing women. They would never get answered.

The gritty street was lit up, but not by neon. Lights on an Emergency Medical Unit's rig slashed the dim evening. A barely visible EMT slung a medical case through the rig's opened rear doors. Sams sat propped outside on a gurney beneath the Neon dancer and her questionable bolts. Rick blocked the slow to rapid flashes of the rig's lights when he stepped in front of Sams.

"Thanks, man." Sams said in relief. The EMT treating Sams then blinded him with a pen light to his eyes.

"No sign of concussion." The EMT said and pocketed her light.

Rick now clearly saw Sams held a mass of gauze over an already bandaged head with his left hand. His right hand was curled into a tight fist at his side. Dried blood clung to his head.

"You a friend of his?" The EMT asked.

"Close enough," Sams answered for him.

"What's the prognosis, doc?" Rick asked.

"He's okay." The EMT said. "He refuses to take a ride to the ER. So watch him."

"I guess you're going to need this back." Sams said and hoped off the gurney.

The EMTs swept up the opened bandage packs, loose equipment, and the gurney in swift precise actions. The rear doors clunked shut and the rig rolled down the road. Rick thought they could have turned off their flashing lights before they rounded a corner. He turned to Sams with blinking eyes.

Rick noticed the shattered front door. "Looks like you had company."

"Not the paying kind." Sams said.

"You call the cops?"

"I called 911 when I recovered," Sams relaxed the pressure of the gauze ball on his head. Several pieces stuck to the wound as he lowered his hand. "I didn't tell them about the B-and-E because then the cops would come first."

"And you needed a medic more than hard questions and a band aid—if the cops would give you a band aid. But now the EMTs will call the cops."

"Yep. But I'm legal. Pretty much."

"Who broke in?"

Sams stopped himself from shrugging and groaned in pain but answered. "No clue. They didn't even steal any cash or booze. Only files."

"Files?"

"Yeah. I need to call the girls, the ones with addresses and numbers."

"Can you describe these guys? I'm sure there was more than one."

"Big fuckers. About five." Sams looked down at his still-clenched, right fist. "I guess I have one clue."

Sams lifted his right fist to Rick and opened it. Inside his palm was a torn epaulet. Sams noticed Rick's eye get wide.

"Tell you anything?"

"A lot."

"I guess. Now you look worse than me."

"I might get worse," Rick grunted in another kind of pain. "You look okay, so I've got to go."

Rick turned and walked away.

"Hey, you know these guys?" Sams called after him.

Rick turned back. "And you don't, and that's good. Board up, heal up, and forget this happened. They got what they wanted. They won't be back."

Rick sprinted to his car with thoughts of Gina Tanner, and Brenda.

SEVEN

Rick's heart raced as fast as his car's pistons fired. He floored it through the streets and intersections not likely to have speed traps. He was expert at avoiding tickets, but had no idea what to do now. The Russian mercenaries were following his playbook, just slightly behind him. And if he could find former dancers from Sams' joint, they would, too. He feared they would not just rattle her.

Rick had no real idea how to save her. Call Bibi? Then what if the mercs weren't there? Call the cops? And say what? That a person of interest in a hooker's death is worried about another one? If he got to Brenda soon enough, he could warn her and she could disappear, maybe into the Golden Horizon.

What confused him was how they treated Joannie. They could've taken her and killed him. They didn't do either. Why? Still, all he could think about was trying to stop Brenda from getting killed like Gina. Maybe the mercs did that. Maybe not. But he had to warn Brenda.

Rick was too late.

The Russians were calm. They sat around Brenda's Rococo style parlor. Only one looked slightly annoyed as he rubbed his fingers from slight shocks he had received when rewiring elevator controls and a few magnetic locks. Another massaged his shoulder under a ripped jacket that was missing an epaulet. Otherwise, they seemed comfortable and in control. Their relaxed nature didn't hide the fact Brenda was their prisoner. She was terrified.

"I'm telling you, relax!" The Russian leader smiled as he sat on the footstool that matched the plush, velvet chair where he effectively trapped Brenda.

All she wore was her silk, morning robe that she managed to don before the mercenaries simply walked in to invade her highly styled world.

"All you need to do is tell me where to find Ekaterina Krymménos." He continued. "Then we go."

"But I don't know who that is!" Brenda curling into a ball in the chair.

"Well, hey, I get loyalty." The leader spoke with a reassuring tone and nodded his head. He looked up and around him with lifted hands and then focused back on Brenda. "I mean this place, huh? This place is special. She treats you special. Now, to save all this, you just tell me—answer me my question."

Brenda pulled her body tighter. She thought and an idea came to her. "Do you mean Car—?"

A buzz came from the pocket of the mercenary rubbing his fingers. He snatched his phone from his breast pocket. He glanced at the screen and spoke the leader.

"*Zhukov, u nas yest' kompaniya.*"

The recently humiliated Anthony Oliver Cord was going to pull up stakes in the city and relocate. He would never again have a night where a stranger forced him to kiss his own ass. At least not in his own house. But before he moved, he was going to take everything he wanted with him. That included the woman he knew as Vera Marie. To make sure no one at the Gemini Towers got in the way and that Vera came with him, Cord had hired a squad of suited security in trench coats. He trusted the online brochure that advertised their personnel as well trained and armed.

As Rick ran around to the maintenance bays, he glimpsed Cord and his trench-coat goons charge into the main lobby.

"Not good!" Rick shouted to himself.

He didn't stop to see Jones. He leapt into the service elevator. The codes still worked. He punched in the floor number and hoped his elevator car was faster. The distance between the main elevators and Brenda's door was a shorter sprint than from Rick's service elevator. That distance saved his life. Cord stayed near the elevators as his trench-coated muscle went to retrieve his passion. Two of the crew saw a wall panel pop open and Rick spill into the hall. It made them draw their guns. Rick threw up his hands.

Inside Brenda's room, someone saw the guns and didn't answer the door kindly. Bullets blasted through the pale blue door. Some of Cord's security crew dove clear. Red craters pocked others as automatic, armor piercing rounds ripped through them. Blood flecks spattered the wallpaper as they fell.

Cord screamed, but less door blocking sound meant louder gun blasts from inside Brenda's room. The trench-coated men that dove away rolled and returned fire with customized Sig-Sauer P226 models. New holes punched into the walls around the shattering door.

Magazines emptied. There was a half-second of peace. The typically lavender scented hallway now smelled of bullet-singed air and the hot mist from super-heated copper and lead blasted through expensive trench coats and tailored suits. Rick felt one or two hammering heartbeats.

It wasn't over.

The mercenaries inside Brenda's apartment fired again and dead on target even through the walls. The surviving trench coat gunmen convulsed and fell. Their dead weight was pulled by gravity but pushed at weird angles by the high-velocity rounds fired from inside.

Rick would see the conclusion of the firefight on security camera video later shown to him by Harou Jones. By the second assault, Rick had hauled his ass back into the hidden elevator.

In the hall, the last of Cord's crew had stood beside him. Now he fired into the apartment. More holes exploded from the wall. His Heckler & Koch MP5K held more bullets than the P226 magazines. He cut a sudden, violent line towards the shattered door as he ran backward to the elevators. He punched the button and dove into the elevator car before its doors fully opened then flattened himself against the side as they closed.

He'd live to fight another day, or maybe rethink his line of work and then get a job as a plumber.

Cord was still screaming, although his lungs were nearly out of air. Strangely, a mercenary from inside carefully opened the shattered remains of the door. As they left, the Russians paid almost no attention to Cord. They secured their compact but now hot Ingram M10s beneath their dated jackets and calmly walked over the bodies and down the hall.

Eventually, Brenda popped her head into the hall to look at the immobile and now weakly mewling Cord. She shook her head in disgust, but the sight of the shot-up goons made her recoil into the room. If EMTs or maybe psychiatrists ever got Cord to calm down, Rick wondered if he would ask the security company for a refund.

As he fled, Rick nearly ran into the last of Cord's goons as they bolted from different doors into the parking garage on street level. The hired gun ran for the light and down the sidewalk at full tilt. Rick guessed the man aimed to run all the way back to the office. Rick later thought he should've asked for his gun. He was likely done with it for the day. Rick might need it where he was heading.

The shoot-out gave Rick a dark opportunity. The need for the Russian mercenaries to flee the hotel and regroup gave him a dark opportunity. If they were hold-up at the Four Winds, they would rendezvous there and confirm it as their base, at least for a few minutes more as they grabbed their spare ammo and gear.

They might also do something to show whom they worked for, such as a phone call, an IM, or an actual meet up. Rick would not follow them from the hotel. He would get there, hopefully, without them seeing him. Then he would take up surveillance.

As an afterthought, Rick figured someone else would call the cops at the Gemini Towers. Maybe Brenda or the housekeeper on her next visit to the hall. There was plenty to clean up.

Rick turned on his car radio. He hoped the sound of music or voices would quell the ringing in his ears or distract him from it. A newscast played.

"—could reach into the billions. Genevieve Elle d'Angevin released a statement downplaying the financial crisis. d'Angevin is the first woman to inherit the title of Bailiff of Alden, making her the technical head of state for the semi-independent bailiwick in the Channel Islands."

"What the hell is a baly-lick?" Rick muttered and clicked off the radio. Rick figured a person like this d'Angevin—an icy sensation shot through his body. A person like d'Angevin could afford mercenaries. The best. From anywhere.

"Shit!" Rick shouted at the idea as he floored his gas pedal to beat a yellow traffic light.

"No way!" he began to argue the possibilities in his head. His car squealed as he turned hard into a grocery's parking lot and hit the brake. He stopped with the engine running. His brain ran faster.

Was the secret madam this d'Angevin? Maybe. Maybe not. Women from the Red Dancer and other places had been disappearing before this financial blow-up began. But it might be connected. And the unseen picture might be big enough to hire mercenaries and even kill over.

The woman pimp that took Gina catered to the rich and ran some hidden club. Maybe Gina saw something she shouldn't have. But she wasn't shot. The morgue photo showed that. But the odds were that someone killed her for a reason. Rick thought of the motives for murder. Sex. Money. And fear. And if you were afraid, you wanted to hide. How deep into hiding do you want to go? Maybe you hid beyond a Golden Horizon.

"Are you here for a grocery pick up?" a young voice asked.

Rick looked up and rolled down his car window. A teenage clerk in a Go Boys! Grocery vest held a stuffed sack of groceries and a smile.

"Yeah. Sure." Rick answered. "That sack got milk?"

"Um, no." the clerk said as he looked in the sack and pushed up a loaf of bread. "There's some cheese!"

"Keep it." Rick said but reached out and swiped the loaf. The clerk looked bewildered as Rick sped off.

Rick wondered if he should go home and shower before he tried his latest plan. He didn't. He wondered if he should pick up a gun. Maybe they sold them at Go Boys! Grocery. He didn't. He wanted to get answers. Fast. He drove to the Astronomy Chateau armed only with his stun gun, air horn, and a loaf of whole wheat bread.

Rick used his Keys-All to bump open the old Plexiglas and aluminum doors to the small lobby of the Astronomy Chateau. His earlier recon suggested the basement level was where the Golden Horizon was hidden. By now, cameras probably told them he was coming. He didn't care. He felt even a squad of mercenaries couldn't stop him. He knew that was bullshit, but didn't think they worked here, anyway.

He walked by doors to bathrooms still marked Boys and Girls with original college signs. Between them sat a closet. Rick went in both bathrooms. They were deeper than the closet. So there was empty space behind the closet, and too much for a wet wall chamber with pipes. Something more was behind the closet's back wall. In the closet, two naked mannequins stood in front of the flanking shelves.

"Yeah," Rick said. "Not that you girls will tell me, but I bet you stark clues are as obvious as two lions by steps. Better, though."

Rick looked for a secret button or switch to open the hidden door. It popped open on its own. Rick looked down beyond the navel of the mannequin on his right and saw the switch.

"Well, young lady, I guess I don't get to know you better."

The back of the closet slide away and reveal a living vision behind it. The vision smiled at Rick, and spoke.

"Hello. I'm Caroline."

The woman blocked Rick and held the doorframe with a sculpted right arm slid out from a burgundy velvet dress that was more a draped robe as if to suggest it might fall away and reveal her shapely body. She was tall. Beautiful. And possessing a regal presence a person would expect from an empress, even one whose subjects were prostitutes and their johns. But she was African American.

Rick looked at her with a wry smile. "No, you're not."

The woman's smile vanished, but she kept up the act. "Dear sir, perhaps you—"

"No offense," Rick took the woman's arm and waist and guided her backwards like an awkward dance move as her muscles stiffened. He let her go, and then walked farther into the Golden Horizon.

Gold highlighted deep-red hues for the walls and furnishings. The hidden club was much bigger than he had guessed. It was as large as a hotel bar, a very posh and well-stocked bar, with the addition of an ornate, half-circle stage. The place was arranged almost like the Red Dancer, if someone dumped a million dollars or more and coffee table book on Art Deco architecture on it. Rick was sure he could get a Bushmills or better, here. Rick noticed closed curtains that concealed a room towards the room's right corner. Rick though that if this bordello with booze had a happy hour, that room likely served to make customers overjoyed.

"Nice place." Rick observed. "Glad I came before the happy hour. Where's the owner?"

Rick turned back to the woman who had greeted him. Now her body and fists were poised and ready to attack.

"I said the owner, not the bouncer." Rick joked, but the fierceness in the woman's eyes made him lean back.

"It's alright, Seline." Another woman said as she entered from the curtained room.

Rick recognized her as the woman he saw in the car with Gina Tanner. She wore the same style of robe-dress, but with a golden lion broach encrusted with jewels low on her cleavage. Rick was sure this was the real Caroline.

"You may go. I'll be fine." The newly emerged Caroline said.

Seline looked at Caroline skeptically. Caroline bowed her head and Seline walked to the bar and disappeared through a passage behind it.

"I am Caroline. Mr. Fredricks. You have been looking for me, even if you didn't know it at the start. You have been traveling a circuitous path across some of my assets."

"The straight line wasn't obvious," Rick said. "And I guess by assets you also mean people, like Brenda. And Gina."

"And more, of course. Such as your dance partner."

"I'd love to see her tango." Rick pointed to the stage. "I hear it's quite a show."

"I can arrange for you to see it," Caroline motioned for Rick to join her in the curtained anteroom.

Rick walked over, but stayed at the doorway against the curtains. A red-velvet daybed, couch, and large, plush chair were inside the room. Caroline sat in the chair and folded her legs.

"Sometimes not being seen is a better idea among some crowds." Rick said. "Sort of like how you make women disappear."

"They come here, and I pay them well." Caroline stroked the arms of her chair. "They can always leave, if they wish."

"Right. One question. Did you kill Gina Tanner?"

"Caroline made a quick laugh. "Shimmer Girl. A dear young thing. No. Of course not. Such an odd question. Why would I?"

"I haven't figured a motive. Yet. But she was murdered."

"Of this you are sure?" Caroline asked but her expression didn't suggest doubt.

"Two cops gave me good reason to think so. So, yeah. I'm sure." Rick was careful not to mention Whilton and Hardin accused him of the crime.

"Maybe they liked you for her death." Caroline taunted.

"Cops like a lot of things. Funny thing, donuts not so much."

"You must spend a lot of time with them."

"You spend time entertaining people in a much different pay scale than cops and public servants." Rick looked back into the main club. "That must get you a lot of friends. And enemies."

"I like donuts." Caroline smiled. He reply seemed to have no context, but her eyes locked on Rick with a playful look.

"I'd have guessed you were more of a croissant girl."

"Yes, well." Caroline nodded. "I do have refined tastes."

"I guess this place allows that. You can probably afford the building. So why rent from Clayton Haines?"

"Well, rent. It's a harsh word. He and I have an arrangement. A—"

"He's your front." Rick said.

"An understanding." Caroline finished.

"And I'm guessing you understand more about the Alden crisis than most. I'm pretty sure you're not this d'Angevin, but—"

Caroline burst into laughter.

"Yeah, I'll call that confirmation. But you are involved. And based on this place, I'm guessing you were her pimp."

Caroline took a long, deep sigh. "Why is it the terriers, the little bull dogs, they bite and just keep pulling and pulling?"

"I guess I'm this dog." Rick resisted calling Caroline a bitch.

"You have debts? Of course. I can make them go away. You didn't indulge with my sweet Shimmer, but take this offer. Stop biting my heels. Be smart." Caroline's tone was terse but she ended with a smile.

"It's been a while since I left teeth marks on anyone." Rick shrugged. "But I want answers. When I know the big picture, then we'll talk numbers. But, information first."

"Alright." Caroline slowly nodded and took a breath. "What do you want, first?"

"The Russians." Rick asked.

"I don't know them." Caroline answered.

"But did you hire them?"

"No."

Caroline's short, quick answer convinced Rick that was true. "Then who did?"

Caroline said nothing and slowly turned her head away. She took a long and shuddering breath. She opened her mouth to speak, but then stood from her chair and began to walk out of the room. She stopped and dropped her head. She was close enough to Rick for him to touch her. He smelled her perfume was a perfect reproduction of fresh roses. Her body started to sway. Rick resisted a gentle caress of the velvet shoulder. It was likely what she wanted. A gentle act of gaining sympathy, but still a power play.

"d'Angevin." Caroline finally answered in a low and actually pained voice.

This time Rick was quiet. The name changed everything. The scale of the case just exploded. But he had to press her for more. "Why? To find you?"

"Most likely." Caroline faced Rick.

He found her as equally stunning as Brenda or Seline. Rick knew his admiration was in his eyes. He needed to use his time with Caroline in ways other than what his body was suggesting.

"I think that means definitely." Rick said. "And, again, why? You must have something big. She's already going down. What could you have to make her life worse?"

Caroline made a slight sigh, and then walked back to her chair. "Financial crises come. And they go. It's what you hold onto between them that lets you survive and perhaps even recover and build. If that something is lost, you are lost."

"So what you have will take that something away from d'Angevin. She'll sink even deeper." Rick said.

"It will destroy her." Caroline said with a nod.

"Okay. What is it?"

Caroline paused again. She took her seat, and sat like a queen and spoke. "Do you know anything about Alden?"

"It's an island." Rick answered. "It's some kind of country that's also part of Britain, I think. So I guess it's also some sort of tax haven."

"More than that." Caroline rhythmically waved her hands for emphasis while still rested her hands on her thighs. "After the challenges to the unity of the United Kingdom, Alden asserted for more independence. They got it. Alden eased regulations on investments and banking, but still held economic ties to the European Union. This gave investors the ability to operate in both the Common Wealth and EU, and other markets beyond typical financial rules."

"So, a sort of quantum state of investing opportunities." Rick offered.

Caroline cocked her head. "Well, I don't think that's quite right, but alright."

"But it's why Alden became popular with big money." Rick furthered.

"Yes."

"And d'Angevin screwed this over." Rick added.

"No. Well, yes. She may well have been involved in unsavory manipulations, but this is not her greatest crime."

Rick's eyebrows shot up. "That thing you mentioned is worse?"

"Yes. Her crimes are far simpler, but their impact is far greater."

"C'mon!" Rick challenged. "Well what the hell did she do? Steal the crown jewels?"

"Yes."

Rick actually felt his jaw drop.

"Not England's royal collection. She stole her families, and also her countries, royal jewels." Caroline explained. "In the Middle Ages, Alden was its own nation. After the Hundred Year War, all they had left was the island. Its prince swore allegiance the English crown to prevent invasion and preserve his own royal line that d'Angevin descends from. Now, the danger to d'Angevin is not being punished for the theft, but the destruction of her reputation. It would ostracize her from the wealthy world she lives in."

"I get it. The truth would make her a pariah." Rick said. "She couldn't spend whatever cash or loot she's stolen."

"Yes. For some, reputation is worth more than life."

"It's worth a lot of money." Rick sniffed.

"Yes. But Alden itself is in danger. This could shatter investors' faith in the nation itself, even if the island is blameless."

"Seems like that's on the line without the crown jewels entering the picture." Rick made a wry frown.

"Perhaps."

"What did the people do before?" Rick asked.

"Mostly tourism." Caroline answered.

"I'll book a flight, later. I bet there is more pressure on d'Angevin from investors and other interested parties to tie loose ends, even if they don't know she robbed the place." Rick pointed at Caroline. "And that brings us back to you. You know all this. She needs to make sure your mouth stays shut. Permanently."

"And she is getting closer."

"Yeah," Rick sighed. "Her mercs are a few steps behind me."

"Do you think they will find the Golden Horizon?" Caroline's tone became anxious.

"Yep. You'd better get a crew of your own. One's that don't like any version of The Alamo." Rick offered.

"And you will help me to do this?" Caroline leaned toward Rick.

"No." Rick said with cold certainty. "The crews I know, I like. I don't want to see them die."

"But you wish me dead?" Caroline's hands formed fists.

"No. But I figure you crossed paths with d'Angevin through your work. Through providing young women."

"I only gave her one woman. Me!"

Those words made Rick pause. "Okay. Can't you use that?"

"No. Again, her reputation is everything. She would not risk me knowing her theft." Caroline took a breath. "I knew this when I discovered it, and so I fled. I never thought she would come across an ocean and continent to find me."

"But a lot of people will know what she did when they pop open Alden's safe."

"No. Not right away." Caroline shook her head, slightly. "She replaced the true jewels and scepter with replicas. Excellent replicas. So long as those are kept under guard, she may live out her life before anyone thinks to test them."

"Nice retirement plan. Or not."

"That is her future." Caroline looked up at Rick with pleading eyes. "I want to save mine. Help me."

"Stay low," Rick said. "And I'd get a ticket out of town."

"How long do you expect me to run?"

"I'm betting this isn't your first game of tag." Rick rolled his shoulders. He thought. "Look, this is going to get worse. You need help, so get it from people who have the power to stop her, to arrest her. Use whatever contacts you have and leak something. Maybe it will slow her down, at least."

Caroline took a breath and looked off considering what Rick had said.

"Crime only pays if you get away with it." Rick offered. "Like you said, when a crime is attached to a famous face, it raises the stakes. Raise hers."

Rick thought he had learned as much as he could. At least tonight. He turned to leave. Another thought hit him, and he turned back to Caroline. "And cut your employees loose. We don't need any more Gina's."

In the street, Rick scanned for people, different cars, especially vans. Maybe he would just see a laser dot. Then the rifle crack would hit his ears in the same fraction of a second the bullet killed his brain. Rick made it to his car. At this hour he could take the scenic route. He would need to check the rearview mirrors more often. Ultimately, tonight had not changed his life much. Yet.

EIGHT

Genevieve Elle d'Angevin loved what she saw. A great track of blue ocean rolled beyond a green plain of flowing grass. In the far distance was France. Her ancient family fled from its coast when forced from the continent. They established their throne on the island now know as Alden. But d'Angevin had no enmity, only love for France. She enjoyed Paris, and to the south Monaco and the Mediterranean. They were her homes as much as the small island with its view of ocean.

Blue ocean stretched to the horizon in every view from her family villa. Her estate remained as European in tastes as it was English. Its influence grew over centuries but never erased the family ties to the Continent. d'Angevin knew the scent of sea air blown though the villa. She knew a white cliff lay beyond the field of green. She recalled—tapping suddenly sounded through the world as it jiggled.

"What?" d'Angevin snapped as she whipped off the virtual reality goggles.

"Hey, you wanted to see me!" The mercenary leader Anton Zhukov said with a shrug. He stood over her with a mass of folders stolen from Sams.

d'Angevin sat up on the bed in the upstairs room of the townhouse. She took a breath, and hated the air.

"Where is Krymménos, or Caroline!" d'Angevin demanded. "It can't be that hard to find her."

"Hey, I think we're doing good. We've been here only days. And now we have more to work with." Zhukov flexed the mass of folders in his hands.

"Those leads brought you into a fire fight."

"Hey, we won. No one has traced us. No worries."

"Any more events like that and you *will* be worried, worried about your reputation and who will hire you after I terminate our contract." d'Angevin said as she stood from the bed.

"Hey, what would you do without us?"

"I would hire more like you. Perhaps better." d'Angevin said and took a step away to put distance between them.

"*Nyet!* None better." Zhukov said with real annoyance. "Besides, you got us through many channels. Not a channel island, eh?" He laughed.

"I grow tired of your plebeian jollity." d'Angevin growled.

"Now, some English I don't get. Did you make a joke?"

"No."

"Well you should." Zhukov smiled, attempting to defuse the tension. It had the opposite effect.

"Be quiet! Just do your job and don't aggravate me!" d'Angevin screamed.

"Now you see, *that* I understand."

"And you need to—"

"Hey, cool off. We are doing our job. And you, you need to be grateful we have taken your contract."

"*I* am to be grateful to *you*? I employ you! You work for me!"

Zhukov took a deep breath and shrugged. "And you got my crew because you know certain people in certain places, and without them, you may already be destroyed. It might be a team like mine that gets you. We all need to be cool. This is enemy territory. It was you who chose to come to the US with us."

"That is to make sure my interests, and orders! are followed. Just remember, Zhukov, you work for *me*!"

"Yes, of course." Zhukov said and left the room. On the stairs, he thought: *if saying so shuts you up, fine. Because if I kill you now, my men don't get paid.*

Typically, Rick never got up an earlier than he had to. But this morning he hoped he was up before anyone who wanted to see me dead. Being essentially self-employed and running down lowlifes even lazier than him allowed some late mornings. A few punks that Rick had found came after him once they got out of the can. It was never to say thanks for giving them a new direction in life, and unfortunately, some of them were morning people. But none of them had the skills of foreign mercenaries, whom also had the skills to plant a well-hidden car bomb. But Rick was drowsy and wanted to speak with Bibi before too much of his office's questionable coffee made him less likely to listen to than normal. Rick trusted his car alarm and security video. It seemed no one had messed with my car. He hoped this trust didn't get him killed.

In Bibi's office, Rick faced similar dangers. He sat at the edge of the chair. He expected Bibi to explode. Rick had told Bibi about his encounter with Caroline. He thought Bibi would see it as a distraction from finding Antoine Everson, whose connection to the Russian mercenaries was only Rick's lie. Now he knew they worked for d'Angevin, but he let the lie persist to keep Bibi as a potential ally against the mercs. He let the link between them and Caroline remain murky.

He told Bibi the mercs shot up the Gemini Towers and likely stayed at the less-luxurious Four Winds. At least he hoped they still rented their townhouse. There wasn't news of a police raid there, or anywhere. Bibi's reaction surprised Rick. He didn't drawn a gun and shoot him. He didn't even yell.

"Okay, PI. That's some bit of digging." Bibi said. "This city has more rotten layers than it you'd think."

Rick wondered how Bibi could think that, considering the work they both did.

"But it sounds like that as you've been digging this stuff up you've also been digging a hole." Bib continued. "I'm not sure I want to dive in with you."

"But you said if the mercs come around—"

"That's different. That's a reaction to provocation. I can hit them if they try to hit me, or me through you. Get it?"

"Sort of a self-defense thing." Rick offered.

"Right." Bib nodded. "If they come for you, call us and we'll take them out. But I can't raid some whorehouse without paper saying I have a right to a bounty. Your Ruskie friends need to be wanted—by the law. By bondsmen. Hell! They need real identities, or something I can track. Best thing is to dig up some identity for your pimping girlfriend—after you nail Everson! Then we can take her in. Maybe."

"I doubt she be happy about that." Rick said.

"If these Ruskies are out for her, jail is a better place than a slab in city morgue." Bibi countered.

"Yeah. But—" Rick stopped. He was about to say she was not the one killing people. But someone killed Gina. Caroline sent Gina and the cops had video. He first thought Gina died from seeing something in Caroline's employ. Maybe that was the truth. But maybe it was something Caroline didn't want her to see.

"Geez. Morning ain't your thing." Pete said as he leaned into the office and noticed Rick lost in thought.

"He's fantasizing about a hooker." Bibi chuckled.

"I'm fantasizing about coffee." Pete said.

"Then too bad you're here." Rick turned his head to Pete.

"Okay comedy man, you have places to be other than here." Bibi said to Rick. "We're done."

Zhukov led his crew up the street to the Astronomy Chateau. The only star visible was the sun. Although, even hours after sunset, star-gazing was near impossible in the city even before LED streetlamps lit public roads and obscured the night sky. As Zhukov and company neared the main entrance, the healed-up, opinionated, likely racist, and apparently stupid security guard stepped out to intercept them.

"Hold it right there!" the guard barked with a hand out to block them. He noticed their similar jackets, although one now wore a blazer. "Are you guys some kind of group?"

"Group?" Zhukov asked. "Yes. Obviously."

"I mean like a band!" The guard scoffed.

"Hey, yeah. We are a singing group. The Igor Butman sans sax band. And we are going in there."

"No you're not!" The guard shook his head and reached for his empty mace holster.

"Hey, you are a little overmatched, eh? Be cool. Maybe we'll give a tambourine." Zhukov laughed.

"Or let you keep your teeth." The tall man in a blazer said clearly, but with a heavier accent.

Zhukov, the leader smiled. His men walked around him and continued to the building.

"But you can help me." Zhukov said. "The doors are locked, no?"

"Yeah. Of course." The guard said looking at the passing men, nervously.

"Then give me your key." Zhukov held out his hand.

"Wait! I can't—"

Zhukov lost his smile and pushed the guard backward against the building wall. His men doubled back and surrounded them.

"I'm not paid enough for this!" The guard pulled out a magnetic-strip keycard and tossed it up to Zhukov.

"Hey, nice." Zhukov caught the card and walked to the doors. His crew kept the guard against the wall.

"What?" The guard protested. "I gave you the key!"

"Hey, first we see if works." Zhukov smiled. "Then you get fired."

Rick tried to sit in darkness, but the sun refused to move faster. As light streamed though his window blinds, he considered his next moves. The attempted frame job was unresolved. His freedom was subject to the whims of detectives Shrinkage and Boner, also known as Whilton and Hardin, and how much pressure they were under to make an arrest. Gina Tanner's record probably put her murder at the bottom of their collective agenda. Sick, but it gave Rick some time.

If he could work an angle in time—he probably couldn't. The Russian mercenaries were on the move, but they did leave Brenda alive. Maybe he could give them what they wanted. If they caught him. Maybe he should just go on the run. But without the cash like in Caroline's pockets, it would be a short jog. The thought of Caroline reminded him that one person had the means to set him up and a connection to Gina. Another thought kept coming back. His ass was close to the edge and he didn't like the draft from the bottom of the cliff. Maybe he—

There was a knock at the door. Time was up.

Rick looked at his security camera's feed, and the closed his laptop. He thought of just ignoring the knock. It repeated. Slowly he went to the door and opened it. The crux of an international crisis was there at his crummy apartment door.

Caroline locked at Rick plaintively and then said "the mercenaries."

"Okay," Rick sighed. He stepped aside to let her in.

The velvet dress was gone. Now Caroline wore street clothes, if from labels too posh for Rick's local department stores, or worn by anyone Rick had ever known before now. Rick did expect her to wear high stilettos revealing painted toes, but Caroline wore vamped pumps but with jacked platforms.

Caroline carried a small travel bag that sagged under the weight of its contents. Rick reached for it but Caroline shifted her grip away from his hand. She dropped it beside the bar counter that framed his apartments quarter kitchen by stretch of tiled floor Rick called spider alley.

Caroline rounded the counter, and sat on a stool. She appeared to relax. Rick felt he needed help to do that, and reached in his refrigerator. He had meant to clean it out since last year's holidays. One day he would find that tub of leftover gravy. Unless it had left on its own. He took two cans of beer and popped them open. Rick thought of the well-stocked bar at the Golden Horizon. Now its owner sat on his bar stool with torn seat and drank his cheap-ass beer.

A spike of fear shot through him. He was afraid she asked to use the toilet. It needed a good scrub. Hell, so did he.

"They came into the Astronomy," Caroline continued. "But so far they have not found the Golden Horizon."

"But they will." Rick added as he leaned against the once-plush recliner he got when his dad moved. His dad was still expecting it as his new place.

"Yes. And that's why I came here."

"No rich clients with a spare room."

"None that I can trust. And I'm sure their wives and other mistresses would be thrilled to have me as a guest." Caroline said with a straight face, but it wrinkled as she took a sip of beer.

"And I guess Motel Sixty is booked up?" Rick said and took a deep pull from his can.

"I don't know that place."

"Just as well." Rick shrugged. "At least in this town."

"Expensive?"

"Ah, no. I just don't think they steam cleaned after a series of murders. You just know all that blood is just a stain under the carpets."

"That is horrible." Caroline said.

Rick was fairly sure she meant the motel murders, not his beer.

"Yeah. But, they still have free ice."

Caroline looked at her beer. "We could use some now."

"I could use a better brand. But, that would be expensive."

Not as expensive as the mercenaries Genevieve has hired." Caroline said and took a long sigh.

"Who?"

"Genevieve Elle d'Angevin." Caroline answered.

"Right." Rick took a deep pull from his own can. He knew d'Angevin was now quickly becoming a powerful enemy of his, as well. And maybe he was sharing beer with another.

"I will need a place to stay." Caroline looked across the apartment. Her expression suggested she was reconsidering her plan to stay with Rick.

"Yeah, well—"

"I assume you have a double bed." Caroline said with her eyes locked on Rick.

Rick grunted. "Look, if you need a new hiding place, try Mars. It's nice this time of year."

"You mock." Caroline said coldly and stood from her stool as she berated Rick. "And you kill, through inaction. But just as certain as the mercenaries!"

Rick gave no reply and Caroline pressed her point.

"You said the mercenaries were a few steps behind you. So you are the one who can keep me ahead of them. Or you can put me on the street and see me die, just like Gina."

"You are nothing like Gina." Rick growled.

"No? I doubt you knew her well. Maybe not all."

"I knew her parents. Still, do. Technically."

"You worked for them?"

"Yes."

"You took money from them. So I guess you and Gina, and you and I are a little alike."

"Not quite." Rick took a half-hearted sip.

"Perhaps not. But perhaps, in a way. You feel some guilt to Gina? Her parents?"

"Yeah. Of course." Rick sighed and wished he still had that bottle of Bushmills.

"But do you morn Gina herself, or do you morn the image you made of her? Your ideal of her? I knew her as a real person. I took her in. I took care of her."

Rick thought of the other definition of the phrase as he considered Caroline.

"She and I had a similar origin."

"So you danced at strip clubs?" Rick said with a wry smile.

"Yes. Does that shock you?"

"I suppose not. But you got yourself far away from clubs like the one you took Gina out of."

"Yes." Caroline said with a hint of pride. "And perhaps Gina could have gone as far. We will never know. But I know you can help me. And I ask you, please, help me."

Caroline looked at Rick and thought herself she had not convinced him. But she could still gain his help through a practiced skill. Seduction.

"I can still dance," she said. "Would you like to watch?"

"Well, I can't cha-cha, personally."

"You only have to sit. Go ahead. Sit." Caroline went to Rick and took his beer. She put it on the stool. She guided him into the recliner with a gentle push. "You know you want to see me dance. Let me. What could it hurt?"

What could it hurt? Rick thought. One hundred reasons why this was a bad idea might have come to his mind, but Caroline was already in motion. Her body went from gently swaying with a smile to suggestive, upward waves with expressions of ecstasy. Rick had upward sensations as blood pumped hard and thoughts of surging motions took on their own momentum. Caroline's complete striptease only solidified Rick's desire.

She pushed him back in the chair and kissed him. Rick thought that if this went any further, his dad would never get the chair back. He wouldn't. Caroline's face slid down as her hands unbuckled his belt and unzipped his pants. Subtle fingers parted his plaid boxers. Rick's eyes watched the top of her head move up and down. He felt her hair caress his hips as he felt the oral expertise of her lips and tongue. Then suddenly, she yanked down his pants and shorts to reveal his all, naked, wet and erect.

His pants and belt wrapped his ankles like a loose rope restricting him. Maybe she planned that. She wanted to be in control. Rick did not protest. She gripped his arms and slid her body over his. She leaned her head next to his for stability as she straddled him with her legs. Her hair covered his face as she reached between her legs and guided their union. She eased over him and slid down until they joined at the hips.

She bit his ear and licked his cheek as she lifted her head and threw it back as she began to find a rhythm. The action pressed Rick and his rumpled shirt deeper into the chair. He strained against the ebbing light to watch her shapely, ample, breasts gently undulated.

Later in his bedroom, Rick tore off his shirt but left the lights on. He knew, compared to Caroline, his motions were crude forceful, and over-eager. Even so, each time it was Caroline who did not protest.

NINE

Rick was early to rise again. Caroline stayed asleep as he showered, shaved, cleaned his toilet, and dressed. He mused over granola that he ate dry, without milk.

The case that started with finding a lost daughter turned exotic dancer, turned high-end call girl, turned murder victim now involved an international thief, a potential murder charge against him, and the material witness and high-priced madam linked to it all and in his bed.

The biggest issue, to Rick, was avoiding arrest. He needed more information to clear himself but that might indict the woman who he had sex with through the night. He thought of the phrase 'it's complicated.' But the two of them straining the recliner springs and his already collapsed mattress was not complex. It was animal lust. Now, human concerns took him over.

Rick nodded to himself, and looked down at the bag Caroline had brought in. He lifted it to the bar counter. It was heavy. And locked. Rick didn't need his Keys-All to pop the small padlock. Inside were smaller pouches with expected travel supplies and toiletries. One held jewels.

Some gems were loose. Others adorned gold broaches, necklaces, and rings. Rick recognized the lion head broach Caroline wore at her hidden club. Together they created a spectrum of expense from onyx to diamond. One emerald ring caught his eye. His picked it out of the pouch. The ring holding the emerald was the most luminous gold Rick had seen. The large, green gem reflected the morning light and let it ricochet inside it. The ring was brilliant gold and mounted with a very precious gem, but it looked crudely made for such high-end materials.

Rick looked up from the ring and at the glaring Caroline. She wore only his torn short from last night. Rick thought she looked odd, even without her glare, with messed up-hair.

"Do you always break into a guest's personal property?" She asked.

"Under the circumstances, yeah." Rick said. "Want another beer?"

"No." Caroline said and reached into the bag to retrieve her toiletries pouch and fresh, French-cut panties.

"You'll have plenty of time to rifle through the place while I'm gone." Rick said.

Caroline turned with a look of worry replacing her glare. "Where are you going?"

"To risk my life to prove a point," Rick said and slipped on his jacket. "While I'm gone, you need to think about what and how to release—I guess leak some info to turn up the heat on d'Angevin. We need to make her boys slow down by tripping her up."

Caroline sighed and looked across the apartment, as if lost. Rick went to work.

Rick left CCS with a bag of his own. Bibi might prove to be good for protection from mercenaries, but he was for sure good for decent equipment. Rick had collected a tool kit of surveillance gear. He carefully avoided Bibi's eyes, and hoped he didn't check the internal camera feeds.

Rick went to play a long shot. He returned to the Four Winds to watch, and with the help of amplified electronic ears, listen. If he just picked up a few phrases in Russian, he hoped to get them translated and hoped on top of that they proved incriminating to them and liberating for him.

And maybe some would hit a number to phone d'Angevin and he could record it from button tones or catch a signal that let him find a *back*door.

It was all a long shot with lousier odds than winning the super-ultra-mega lotto. But, he bought a ticket and looked for a good hide to set up. The 'De La Rosa Professional Campus' was hardly a fitting tag for the place Rick chose. There were no roses, anywhere. The 'Weeds in Cracks Abandoned Building' fit better. It was almost a straight shot across from the Four Winds. Rick parked behind a rusting truck and grabbed his gear.

The 'De La Rosa' was an industrial site before mean-spirited or stupid developers converted its buildings into cheap, drafty office space. The metallic sterility of the complex made it hard to find renters, even before the pandemic. Afterwards, the building stayed abandoned. Squatters found other digs. Even rats favored other places. Spiders, always plentiful in late summer, took up the job of populating the lot and interior. There didn't seem to be much for the spiders to catch in webs or ambush on the ground. Rick assumed they eventually ate each other. You needed to make a living, somehow.

Rick needed his freedom to pay rent, and eventually get milk. Recently, sex was free. Not that it ever entered his loosely figured budget. The gate and door locks were also loose. Rick was cautious and practiced in avoiding tails in cars or on foot. The person who locked onto him was slightly better. Still, Rick caught the soft echo of leather soles against pavement grit after the jangle of a dropped locking chain against the metal gate stopped.

Rick ticked off several spiders as he tore through their webs rolling through a window he found ajar. The window was hidden in plain sight. The side of the building was all sections of Plexiglas. When he closed the window, all the panes looked the same. Rick ducked behind a vinyl curtain that smelled like mildew growing mildew, but he ditched his tail. Rick waited for the moment to get a good look at him.

Rick tried to slow his increased heart rate. He assumed his tracker was a lonely security guard he might bride just with pleasant conversation. He really hoped so. No luck. Security guards, even ones that didn't wear uniforms, never wore suits, ties, and nice raincoats to patrol. And no one around the city wore a trilby style hat. Who the hell did?

The man looked around and cased the side of the building. Rick eased back slightly from the stinking vinyl just in case his rapid heartbeat started the curtain to flutter. He checked the angle of the sun to avoid a reflected flare of sunlight, and then peered through his sniper scope. He saw the narrow faced, middle-aged, and white face take on a disappointed frown. The man turned and walked back toward the street. Rick found a stairway. And more spider webs.

From the second story, Rick saw the man stop by the rusting truck. He knew Rick's car behind it was a new addition to the landscape. Damn. The man in the raincoat took out his phone. Rick took out the compact sound gun. He picked up accented speech from under the trilby and the other voice on the phone. Rick surmised the actions of the man were those of a cop. The voice on the phone was, for sure.

Whilton's voice was clear. "...last thing he did was make nice with a local hooker."

"Is he wanted?" the unknown cop in the trilby hat asked with an accent certainly not from the South.

"Sort of." Whilton answered. "But there's isn't enough to stuff him. Yet. If you find Fredricks, don't tell him that."

"Of course not. We are professionals."

"Right," Whilton said. "Well, *say la voi.*"

"What? Do you mean *c'est le vie?*"

"Yeah. Ain't that French for good bye?"

"No. This is." The French detective just hung up.

Rick smiled. His joy was short lived. He assumed the French detective was an Interpol agent investigating either the mercenaries or d'Angevin. So maybe she was close. But he didn't think it would be as easy to get away with stunning an Interpol agent as a local rent-a-cop. He would now have to leave his car here, for now. Few ride shares would come out to the area. Rick would have to take the bus. He hated the bus.

Zhukov did something he hated. He was capable of a great many things. Some of them most people found horrifying. But he approached every task with calm assurance. But despite all his combat and interrogation training, he felt dread as he walked up the steps of the Four Winds townhouse. He entered the bedroom without knocking. Genevieve Elle d'Angevin would yell at him for something, anyway.

"Have you found Krymménos?" she asked but did not look up at Zhukov as she read from a laptop screen while sitting on the bed.

"I think so," he answered.

"You think so? Not good enough!" d'Angevin slammed the laptop closed and looked up at Zhukov with a harsh stare.

"No." Zhukov nodded. "But we will. Right now—"

"Right now you will march out and bring me Ekaterina, or Caroline, Krymménos!" d'Angevin gnashed her perfect, white teeth.

Zhukov admired her dental work for a half-second, and then continued. "Sure. Sure. But look, boss, you need to listen to me."

"Once again you try my patience with your peasant antics! You—"

"You know what?" Zhukov cut on with a rarely raised voice. "You can do I as I suggest, or I can shoot you here."

"What?" d'Angevin screeched.

"Got your attention, now. Good. Listen." Zhukov spoke in his typical, calm tone. "Someone has been watching this place. Someone good. But something made them leave their position to investigate it, and we caught a glimpse of them. So, we need to prepare. All of us."

"Then why didn't you just say that?"

"Hey, I tried, but you were too much of a bitch."

Rick stood near the street, his apartment house and an uncertain future loomed near. He knew his digs were ultimately not good enough for a well-paid madam. Caroline already looked ready to bug out despite the danger of being spotted. But his address was safe enough for a Swift ride share. The name Swift was ironic. He could have had another cup of coffee. It would prove good that he didn't.

In order to return to the Four Winds, he would need to do surveillance of the place he wanted for surveillance. If no one was around to do surveillance of him, he could at least get his car.

Rick finally saw an Audi with a Swift sticker roll closer. Rick never got to climb in. His heart became numb and cold. His blood didn't suddenly chill to ice water. It became shards of glacier. Bibi's asphalt-grey, hybrid SUV sped down his street followed by another.

Rick thought of Caroline in his apartment. Maybe an indictment had came down for her and Bibi came with the full force of the Hazardous Offenders Team to apprehend her and collect what someone posted as a major bounty. Or maybe they came for him. Or maybe the photo he shot at the Four Winds after the French agent left had hit pay dirt.

He had needed to wait for the Interpol agent to be elsewhere before he could leave. So Rick spent several hours scanning the townhouses. Finally, a curtain parted in a second story room. A blonde woman glanced out for less than a second. But it was more than enough for Rick's digital cameras' shutter speed and long-range focus. Having an interesting trek home, Rick encoded and sent the images to CCS. Rick thought the woman might be one of Caroline's stable perhaps captured by the mercenaries. He had no idea she was Genevieve Elle d'Angevin, herself.

Bibi's Range Rover cut off the Audi and sped up to Rick. Bibi threw open the driver's side door and leapt out. He raced around the front of the SUV as the passenger door opened. Rick saw Rusty glare from the back seat.

Bibi looked at the bewildered Rick and pointed to the driver's side. He yelled "get in!"

Rick sprinted to the SUV, although his legs felt gelatinous from relief that his apartment, and Caroline, would stay intact.

"Okay, what, where—?" Rick began as he slammed the door shut.

"This Four Winds Bar!" Bibi cut in.

"Ah, it's more like a hotel." Rick said. "Sort of."

"Get us there." Bibi ordered.

Rick was already racing toward the main avenue. "Okay."

Rick waited for Bibi to fill him in as he drove.

Bibi only said "faster!"

"We IDed you mystery woman," Rusty said from behind Rick. "She's wanted. Big time."

"I guess she's a major target." Rick said. "You bringing in HOT to control traffic?"

"No." Bibi answered waving his hand like a foot on a gas pedal. "I'm bringing them in to kill off the goons she might have with her. It's that bitch Genevieve d'Angevin. She's—"

"Shit!" Rick yelled. "Bibi, she's the one—"

"Behind the mercenaries new in town," Bibi finished. "I figured. The two parties in the same city at the same time is no coincidence."

"Bibi, I've seen these guys work. Be careful, man!"

"And for you think we suck at this?" Bibi challenged.

"C'mon, Bibi! I—"

"It's cool, Rick. I'm jerking your chain." Bibi smiled.

"Oh. Trying something new." Rick said.

"Ha-ha," Bibi said dryly. "We need you to get us there fast."

Rick sped through a red light. Vehicles entering the intersection hit their brakes and horns. The CCS SUV following Rick kept pace right behind him. Bibi smiled at Rick's driving.

"GPS can get us there, but I'm sure you have scoped the place out." Bibi continued.

"Yep." Rick felt the steering wheel almost pop his thumbs free as the SUV bounced over a shortcut side road with deceptively deep dips in the road. Rick had never driven over them at high speed.

Rick adjusted his grip and pushed the gas pedal farther down. "So this d'Angevin must have a huge bounty."

"Yeah, I'm sure she will." Bibi answered.

"So—" Rick started as the SUVs squealed around a tight turn that sent everyone pressed against the driver's side.

"You're apprehending her on spec?" Rick finished.

"Like you say: sort of." Bibi answered making Rusty smile.

"Is it legal?" Rick asked almost grazing a pick-up and then swerving to miss a vintage, year 2000 Camaro.

"You working for the feds now?" Bibi asked as his body pitched left then right.

"Nope."

"Then shut up and drive." Bibi yapped. "When we get there, drop us at a spot where we can deploy."

"Good luck," Rick said with sincerity.

"We won't need it." Rusty said from the back.

Rick glanced in the rearview mirror at Rusty who was not glaring at him as he thought. Rusty was staring out at the road and almost looked pensive. Rick said nothing, and drove.

TEN

Near the Four Winds, Rick instinctively switched over to the quiet all-electric mode. From the lack of sound, he understood the following SUV had already done so. He pulled almost silently into the De La Rosa campus. The other SUV followed. Only the sound of gravel under tires betrayed their entry. The vehicles stopped by the side of the building and out of sight from the Four Winds across the street. Rusty and Bibi were already out the SUV in the time Rick reached for his door handle.

At the back, Rusty opened the rear door. He and Bibi ripped off their street jackets and whipped on the black, woven armor tunics the maker said was better than Kevlar. Rick hoped that was true. They covered the armor tunics with buckled ammo vests, of course also black, and with enough pockets to make them almost look puffy. They clipped belts around their waists with more spare clips and their side arms.

The HOT members in the other SUV moved so quickly when leaving their vehicle the doors didn't appear to open and close. The team seemed to teleport from inside to the ground. Pete was recognizable behind his assault rifle, clad in black and goggles. He gave Rick a quick smile and two-finger salute.

Bibi had standardized weapons and equipment for his team. Each man had the new Glock 50 handgun holstered at the hips of their choice. For their main weapon, Bibi had armed them with the tried and true Heckler & Koch Gewehr 36, C variant. The HKG36C was a compact, light assault rifle developed in Germany and a venerable firearm used by police, military, other private, covert, and possibly criminal forces worldwide. Even with the stock folded, Rick thought they looked like the love child of a machine gun and a jet fighter.

The exception to weapon uniformity was Bibi's long gun. He slung a weapon more massive than the HK assault rifles. It didn't fire bullets but 12-gauge rounds. The Israeli-American origins and firepower of Bibi's Tavor TS12 semi-automatic tactical shotgun were similar to the man.

Despite looking like his rifle was a natural part of him, Rusty's biggest weapon was his glare. Rick felt like the team mascot on the sidelines without a costume. Maybe Bibi had brought a cheerleader's skirt.

"It's number eleven," Rick offered before he was asked to confirm the mercenaries, and maybe d'Avengin's hideout.

"Go to eleven?" Pete said and smiled, but no one but Rick seemed to appreciate his taste in classic cinema.

"Yep. Crank it, and come back." Rick replied.

"No worries."

"Let's go." Bibi said without a raised voice but in a tone heard by all.

"Stay here, out of sight." Bibi ordered and checked his weapon. He and Rusty joined Pete and the other HOT members.

If Rick didn't know where to look, he might not have seen them shoot across the street faster and lower than sidewinders. He wondered if some device gave them semi-invisibility, but he knew such motion was a practiced skill. He felt a drop of pride from the team trust in him not to reveal their presence.

Each unit had a short yard in the front giving it a few feet of weeds between the front door and the street. The Hot crew flew across them to the door of number 11. Rick clutched the building's glass and aluminum corner and peered over to number eleven with one eye. He should have also covered his ears.

Bibi kicked the door open and the HOT crew flew into the townhouse. Even against a trained enemy, surprise was a great advantage especially in a frontal attack. No one in Bibi's crew knew they were expected. Rick felt the pain in his ears as blast inside hurled shards and one of the HOT crew out into the weeds.

Bibi's shotgun sounded as bass beat among the eruption of automatic fire. The noise was not just loud but sharp and painful to Rick's already assaulted ears. The bursts of automatic fire followed the rhythm of an electrical arc. There was another explosion inside the townhouse. Bibi fire two shots. A burst of rifle fire followed. Then, silence.

Rick heard garbled human voice through his ringing ears. Someone was shouting in Russian. Rick expected more gunfire. To his shock, three mercenaries came out of the number eleven. One was their leader. They spoke in calm tones and looked over the fallen HOT member. They walked towards a car across the street. Rick dropped and flattened himself against the grit and concrete foundation. If they saw him, they would kill him. His pounding heart seemed to push him up in a rocking motion. As he held his breath, the Russians drove the other way.

He remembered his car. This could be over for him. He thought of running. He didn't. Rick pushed himself up and looked over at the townhouse. If anyone else was renting in the Four Winds, they were flattened and unmoving in their own units. Rick felt numb as if drugged, but drawn to number eleven.

Even though he saw some mercenaries drive off, he expected to find Pete, Bibi and the gang standing over the bodies of their fallen enemy. The body of the HOT member blown into the short yard crushed that fantasy. The interior smelled like a whole world and any hope blasted and burned.

The explosions were C4 rigged at the front door and at the bottom of the stairs. From the bodies, sprayed blood, and bullets holes, Rick imagined the mercenaries set off the C4 and then attacked from the back bedroom and down the stairs to kill any surviving HOT members. The plan worked. Rick found Bibi at the foot of the stairs. He had led from the front. Pete was across the room lying strangely flat on his back, almost looking relaxed. But his grimaced face and clothing looked burned. Rick felt for a pulse. Nothing.

Even in his shocked state, Rick knew the thought was sick but he was glad to see mercenaries among the bodies. To fight Bibi's crew they had not used their compact M10s. The dead mercenaries also had HKG36C assault rifles, but theirs had bigger drum magazines loaded with armor-piercing rounds that Rick could see were horrifically effective against the 'better than Kevlar' armor. Otherwise, their weapons and gear looked identical to what Bibi provided his HOT crew. Rick wondered if it all came from the same supplier. Money from any source or side all spent the same.

The shock began to ebb and Rick had a moment of clarity. He pulled out his phone and hit 911.

Nothing. His phone could not connect. He ran outside.

Nothing. Somewhere the mercenaries were generating a jamming field. Rick stepped back inside as he uselessly kept hitting 911 on his phone.

Bibi moaned.

Rick shot over to him and rolled Bibi over. Bibi made protesting cries, but eased up when he saw Rick's face. He smiled at his broken, bleeding, and charred boss.

Bibi took a pained breath and said, "You're fired."

Rick shook his head and smiled. "No time for jokes, boss." He said and heard a tremble in his voice.

Bibi almost smiled through his burns and blood. He took another pained breath and jerked his head at the stairs. "Rusty. He's alive. Up-"

Bibi seemed to deflate as he stopped breathing.

Shit! Rick thought.

He slowly stood up from Bibi and then looked up the smoldering and bloody stairs. He thought that if he had any sense he would run and cut his losses. Of course, he didn't. Expecting to get hit by an explosion or a returning mercenary's bullet, he took the first step.

Rick stopped.

He went and knelt back down to Bibi and took his Glock. He began up the stairs again. He stopped. He looked down at the pistol and made sure the safety was flicked off. He remembered it was a Glock with a trigger safety. He sighed, and began up the steps again.

He froze.

"Rebyata, vy tak skoro vernulis'?" came from the top of the stairs.

The mercenary appeared and looked down the stairs holding a rifle. A look of shock took his face as several .40-caliber rounds rocked his body. He fell back.

Rick kept squeezing the trigger. He noticed the slide had locked back. The gun was empty. He had thought he just fired one shot.

He ascended the steps and saw the man he just killed. Rick saw the man's intact face and thought he looked younger than he did. But his chest was pocked by the ten rounds Rick had fired into him. He heard a noise like a chair being jerked.

Rick tucked the empty Glock in his belt and took the dead man's HK. He darted his head to look into the room with the noise. He saw Rusty glare back. They had stripped him to the waist and tied him to a metal and vinyl chair. He again suffered the bloodied look that gave him his nickname. Blood oozed from his wounds as he strained against his bonds.

"Whoa, boss. Just quit—"

"Get me out of this!" Rusty screamed.

The ferocity on Rusty's face made Rick think twice about freeing him. Maybe Rusty would kill him next. But Rusty might kill him still tied to the chair if he didn't. Rick set the gun by Rusty and went behind the chair. He began working the knots in the electric cord that had been torn from a lamp and used as makeshift rope.

"Knife!" Rusty yelled. "Left boot!"

Rick slid his fingers in and withdrew a short dagger from Rusty's boot. It sliced through the cord with ease. Rusty shot up from the chair.

"Geez! The tied you up fast!"

"They're pros," Rusty said. "They know they've got limited time. Even in this district. And they'll be back before we can escape."

"Uh, not if we run right now!"

"They'll just catch us and cut us down in the street. This isn't over." Rusty picked up the HK, dripping blood.

"No," Rick felt an upward gush of stomach acid. "I didn't think so."

"Most of our ammo was spent." Rusty said and looked at what Rick had in his belt and yanked it out. "Why did you pick up an empty gun?"

"It wasn't." Rick replied.

"Right. Good work." Rusty nodded. Blood still oozed from his shoulder.

Rick knew the wound was not through and through. He wondered where the bullet was inside Rusty and how long he had to live.

"So we have is what's left in this clip," Rusty motioned with the HK, and your side arm."

"Um," Rick began but saw Rusty reach down to a hidden pocket at his right calf and produced a clip of the Glock.

"Right." Rick exchanged the clips.

"We used most of our ammo, downstairs." Rusty said. "So did the enemy."

"That's why they left? To get more?"

"No. They want to interrogate me." Rusty answered. "It gives us an advantage. This time, surprise will work. Besides, to end this we need to end their leader."

"d'Avengin?" Rick asked.

"No. The lead Russian."

"What about his surviving crew?"

"These new urban merc units, Russian or not, only the main man knows the big picture. They don't." Rusty explained. "End him and they melt back and look for another boss somewhere. If they live."

"But they killed Bibi. Don't they don't think that about you?" Rick asked.

"They know we operate differently. Besides, they think *I'm* the boss."

Rick dared to look straight at Rusty. "Yeah. I can see that. So, what the hell did they leave for?"

"Ingredients. For an interrogation cocktail."

"A truth serum?"

"Sort of." Rusty glanced at his wound.

"So they went out to rob a drug store?" Rick ducked his head to look in the hall.

"No. You can make serums from stuff at a local pharmacy, or hardware store."

"Hardware store?" Rick looked at Rusty with confusion.

"Bug spray. Rat poison. It all works on the nerves, the brain."

"Geez. What are the side effects?"

"Who cares?" Rusty half shrugged and grimaced. "It's a way to break self-control and get info, pronto."

"Right."

"Now we need to be ready." Rusty brought the HK to his waist. "There are only four."

"Three." Rick grunted.

"Right. Good. One or two will come up here with the leader. We take them on."

"Will these guns be enough?"

"No. the mercs downstairs with have his G-thirty six. The ones that come up will probably, too."

"So what if we shoot our wad up here? How do we stop the guy downstairs from coming up and just shooting us?"

"The weapons we take them from the enemy in ambush."

"Ambush. Right." Rick nodded. "Maybe we should—"

Rick began but stopped as he looked at Rusty. His glare was both intimidating and imploring. Rick took a breath.

"Ambush. Right." Rick repeated. "Or they might find someplace later to ambush and kill us, and you would rather die fighting."

"No. I'd rather fight and maybe not die. I'm a soldier, not a martyr. And right now, you're a soldier. You better fight, or I'll kill you."

"Well, I think I proved I know what end of a gun the bullets come out of." Rick said.

"Then point and shoot when I tell you to."

"Yes, sir." Rick pointed as the large hole ripped in Rusty's shoulder. "That gonna be okay?"

"It will have to be." Rusty motioned to the hall with his good arm. "The body. Hide it in the other bedroom."

"On it." Rick snaked into the hall pointing the Glock.

He secured the gun in his belt and then dragged the man he shot into the opposite bedroom. It had a bed. Rick dragged the body to its side that blocked the line of sight. He took a breath, but didn't notice the man's blood was now all over his clothes. He heard a creak of stairs.

"Hey! Vitali, you American tourist!" The voice was actually calm and playful, and familiar. The leader was back.

Zhukov felt his handgun rub the small of his back as he juggled his serum supplies and walked into the room. He smiled at his defiant captive in the chair. He held a bottle of alcohol and small boxes of everyday toxins for sale almost everywhere that he could mix into a cocktail to give Rusty a very bad night. Zhukov glanced at the closet door. Unlike before, it was now ajar. He dropped his supplies.

Simultaneously, his lieutenant, who was now the only mercenary not in an epaulet jacket, noticed red streaks on the upstairs carpet just as Zhukov had entered the room. He opened his mouth to speak but saw motion in his peripheral vision. He lifted his HK into position as Rick fired the Glock point blank.

In the room, Rusty leapt from the chair just as the supplies hit the floor and the gunshot sounded. In the hall, Rick saw the guns rip through the man in the blazer. The bullets didn't cut through him in slow motion. His body snapped wildly in fast, jerking movements before he dropped.

Rick heard the man downstairs yelling. His heart felt as if it squeezed out all its blood and froze as Rick tossed aside the empty Glock. He frantically wrestled the assault rifle from the bloody bulk of the dead man. He finally just rolled the whole body to aim the gun down the stairs where the lone mercenary appeared with gun aimed up toward Rick, who fired.

An automatic burst perforated the wall over the mercenary's head. He jerked down and rolled into the short hall at the bottom of the steps blocked by a wall.

Rick could hear bodies slam into walls inside the room where Rusty fought Zhukov. He jerked the HK free of the dead man in the blazer. His body tumbled onto the stairs. It didn't roll down but stuck at the upper stairs. Rick could see the soles of the boots.

Rick crouched and aimed down the stairs and waited for the mercenary below to bolt for the front door or return fire. He glanced from the HK's gun sights at the bullet holes through walls. He recalled the shoot out at the Gemini Towers.

"Oh shit!"

Rick dove to the floor as bullets shot up through the wall hiding the mercenary. Most flew though the space right where his torso had been. He pointed his gun with his best guess and fired back with less accurately but with more bullets. His mind reeled from the repeated and incredibly loud gunfire that rattling his skull when he fired. His ears felt as if someone shoved, not by cotton balls, but by smoldering briquettes in them to cut down his hearing. He managed to hear his enemy call to him.

"Empty! Empty!" The mercenary yelled in English. He tossed out his HK and then showed his empty hands. Rick kept his weapon aimed as the mercenary stepped out with his hands up. Rick relaxed and lowered his gun, slightly. The young man shot a hand behind his back, but dropped his tucked M10 as a short burst of three rounds emptied Rick's magazine and ended the deceptive mercenary's life.

Rick strained to listen, but could not hear sound from the room where Rusty fought. He pulled his weapon's locked bolt to release it, and slid it forward. If someone other than Rusty greeted him, he didn't need to know his magazine was empty. Rick entered the room, gun first. Blood slicked the floor. It wasn't all from Rusty's wound. He was motionless and face down on the floor. Zhukov sat propped against the wall and bleeding from repeated stab wounds.

Zhukov's pistol had slid through blood to the opposite wall. It had been wrestled for and then flung aside. The two men then fought hand to hand. Rusty had a knife, skill, but a shot-up shoulder. Zhukov had nothing but full health and training. That proved enough. Almost. Rusty was dead but had made sure Zhukov would catch up to him in whatever race waited after hearts and minds stopped working. For the last mercenary, that was soon.

Zhukov looked up at Rick and panted through his words. "Next room. Jammer. Switch it off."

"In a minute." Rick said and put down his HK as he knelt down beside Zhukov.

Rick noticed something hit his eye. A small spurt of blood shot for Zhukov's chest when he took a deep breath. Rick ignored it, too. "Where is your boss?"

Zhukov pulled up his slack jaw to make a slight smile. He began to shake his head to signify 'no' but stopped.

"I know it's d'Avengin, ultimately." Rick said.

"The bitch." Zhukov replied, with effort.

"I don't know her that well." Rick said.

"G-Good."

"Where is she?" Rick took out his phone and just held it for Zhukov to see.

"Don't know," Zhukov smiled. "For security."

"So she's supposed to call you?" Rick nodded.

"Maybe not now." Zhukov almost laughed but took a dry swallow.

"Do you know what this all about?" Rick asked.

"I tell you, you die."

"Been tried, but I'm the only one making it out of here on my legs, not a gurney."

"Lucky. That's all." Zhukov said, but began panting faster.

"Maybe. But why hire you guys? No offense."

Zhukov started of a laugh, but ended as a gurgled wheeze. "Hey, oldest—oldest reason."

"Just money?"

"Yeah." Zhukov managed to nod as his eyelids drooped.

"Just the electronic scam, or more?" Rick asked.

"More?" Zhukov somehow perked up when considering the question. "Money system. Alden. Bitch, bitch owes."

Rick watched Zhukov fade, and thought. That island crossed into his life from sound bites and headlines into a blood-soaked room.

Zhukov looked over at Rusty's body. "This guy. Saved you. Now no one—ah, yeah."

"He knew his stuff." Rick added.

"Knew—" Zhukov made a short, wet cough. He looked at Rick's phone in his hand. He made an odd, knowing laugh that Rick found it disturbing, and not something he would soon forget.

"Hey, it's okay you didn't make the call." Zhukov said and panted. "I would've died before they made it. Traff—traffic in this town...."

Zhukov's head didn't roll to a side or close his eyes. His body just became noticeably still now that life was gone.

"Pete," Rick said even realizing Zhukov was gone. "He was my friend. Hell, in a way, so was everyone. You killed him. You killed them all. If I thought you were going to live, I'd have picked up that gun and shot you, anyway."

Rick found the jamming unit. He couldn't find an off switch, so he smashed it against the floor. He thought he heard distant sirens, but they could be going anywhere. And they rarely came here. He made an anonymous 911 call before he slipped away. In a small way, it would honor Pete, Rusty, Bibi and all the HOT crew by getting their bodies out of this bloody mess.

ELEVEN

Rick sat in the recliner. Caroline sat in the couch that came with the apartment. Rick drank his cheap-ass beer. He had taken out two cans. Both were for him. He told Caroline what happened at the Four Winds.

When he finished, Rick didn't think about how he expected Caroline to act. She sat and thought across the room covered by bands of light and shadow as the sun set and outdoor lights flicked on. She stood, but didn't walk over to comfort him. She got what she wanted. Indirectly, he did get Bibi and his team to attack the mercenaries. Now his role was played. And over.

Caroline retrieved her bag that she had hidden in the narrow and shallow broom closet. The most likely place to look, Rick thought. Caroline dragged it out. She picked up her phone from the love seat. She at least looked at Rick before she made the call, for a Swift ride.

"I am going back now." She made her call as she walked back to the bedroom.

Rick swirled his can and considered the present and future. The mercenaries were dead. So was his greatest ally. He wondered if CCS would survive. And his freedom was still in question from a bogus rap. But he was alive. The biggest danger was over. For now. At least for Caroline. He thought about shouting 'you're welcome' at the bedroom. He drained his can instead.

A night went by. Rick didn't wait long for company. He noticed a blonde woman right in his 'hood. She was not ready to file for social security, but looked as if she had some experience in life. Rick could zoom in closer with his scope, but he saw what he needed. He had never thought about all the variations of blonde until seeing several of them, lately. This woman's hair had a uniform color throughout. Maybe it came from a bottle, or she wore a wig. Perhaps a disguise? The face-rec app on his phone didn't ID her.

"Cheap crap." Rick muttered. He looked back out his quarter-kitchen window with its fake interior image facing the street.

Her hair was a mere detail. What the hell she was doing on his street across from his apartment was his main interest. He recognized she was doing the same job as Rick, but it looked as though she had a better set of tools she didn't have to steal from her gig-work employer. He pulled over the bar stool and watched.

Surveillance was a boring job that nicely hidden little cameras could do. They could send push notices if they caught someone through better face recognition apps. The PI could hit a button. Get the feed. Then decide if they needed to go to the location, or go back to sleep in a nice warm bed. Nice. And annoying if your budget required a more old school and cold coffee approach.

This PI had other places to be. She had set up her cameras as if looking through her car, and left on foot. No doubt, a partner or ride was waiting down the block. Question was, who did she working for? Maybe the cops in the older sedan knew. They had parked a few hours before the well-healed PI. After she left, they went over and looked inside her car.

Both were recent promotions from uniformed duty. Now in street clothes, one thought that meant a suit and tie. The other thought his clothes from his last year of college were fine. Neither thought they should coordinate to avoid looking like a theater group version of the odd couple. They probably passed one or two cameras and caused an alert. No car alarm, though. You wouldn't want to draw attention to your robo-surveillance platform.

Rick shrugged and decided to call it a night.

The offices of Cross-Coast Securities were open. Bibi's daughter, Amira, was now the owner. Business went on. Grief went concealed. Rick was there to pay his respects, but if Amira offered to cash him out or give him a new contract, he wouldn't balk. The offices were empty. The television was off. Amira worked quietly in her father's office. Rick smiled as he entered. His reception was cold.

"Mr. Fredricks, hello." Amira said. She had her father's stare and emotionless, tanned face beneath pulled back, black hair.

Rick wondered if the shock of her father's death had frozen her emotions. But he would not expect Bibi's daughter to have a fragile personality. Her attitude and posture made her appear forged from steel.

"I'm afraid your association with this bond company is over, Malik." Amira said.

"Uh, why? I've always—"

Amira raised a hand to stop him "Always suggests the past. I have to keep this place going for the future. I'll have to take stock if the doors can even stay open before thinking about hiring a new crew, *and* keeping the office staff on. The contractors, the giggers, you guys—well, I'm sorry."

"You sure it's a money thing?" Rick asked.

Amira looked off and gave a slight, side-to-side nod. "Dad said you were smart. He wondered why—well, let's say he liked you more than he let on."

"Yeah. He was a great boss. I'm sure a true humanitarian." Rick regretted almost mocking Bibi, but his frustration grew. "But then he might have told you to keep me on if he got waxed. But now you're telling me goodbye. It's a theme, lately."

"Sorry to hear that." Amira said flatly and unmoved. "But I can give you a heads up."

"That and a wad of cash might just make me smile."

"Smiles are cheap enough. But you might be worth more as a bounty. Maybe soon."

Rick suppressed a ripple of fear as Amira tapped at her keypad. She flipped the flat monitor around to Rick. He saw his

ID license photo and another taken on the street pasted over a BOLO notice describing Malik Fredricks as a potential suspect in the murder of Gina Tanner and disappearance of Vera Marie Tolwaithe, AKA Brenda Collings.

"Disappearance of—shit!" Rick snapped. "I'm not even listed as armed and dangerous."

"Are you dangerous?" Amira asked, again flatly.

"If I was, if that BOLO had weight, I'd be in lock-up."

"So your freedom is proof of innocence?"

"It's proof that was written by a pettifogger not close to the case."

"Pettifogger. One I'll have to hit search for." Amira turned the screen back to face her.

"Look, I know the cops working the Tanner case. They've already talked to me."

"Friends on the force keeping you in the clear? Maybe that's a contact I can use, here."

"We're not friends. But you can use me here."

"Maybe. After this is cleaned up." Amira jabbed a finger at the screen. "So I guess you got a job after all. Not here, but one I'm sure you see is important before you work anywhere."

"I'd like one that pays." Rick growled.

"Me, too. Have a good day, Mr. Fredricks."

Rick took a breath and tried to sound conciliatory. "People call me Rick. Or sometimes—"

"Licky?"

"No. Not that."

Rick didn't know when the people who owned the house would be back. They probably had a nine-to-five grind during the day. Rick thought their security system was installed by someone looking to rush home that day. Rick figured he had time, now. He chose the place for its short deck off their kitchen. It overlooked the Astronomy Chateau. A bonus was the much better beer in their fridge. He hoped to have time to see if they had any Bushmills before he left.

But his point to the B&E was the deck and its spy angle on Caroline's building. To use it, he hid in plain sight in camouflage clothing. For the near-to-suburb area in late summer, that was a Hawaiian shirt, cargo shorts, and flip-flops. Along with standard issue dark sunglasses, and a hat that shaded his face. But not a trilby.

Luckily, beer was a common vice if anyone looked up and noticed him. He went through four bottles before he saw his target. Caroline left with Brenda and another young woman. All three women looked happy. Just gals out to enjoy life. Brenda had survived in Caroline's world. Would the new girl, a new Gina Tanner? Caroline's new recruits would not expect threats to life as work hazard.

A ride-share Cadillac pulled up and the three women climbed into the back. They would likely be gone for a long time. That made Rick happier than the fancy beer.

He fished out his phone from the side pocket of his shorts. He looked at the number with dread, but hit dial.

Hours later, Rick skipped his cheap beer to enjoy a free bottle of Bushmills. But his evening was not done. He made another call he dreaded. Caroline answered. Her tone of voice suggested that Rick get used to women treating him with frigidity.

"How did you get my number?" Caroline demanded.

"I cloned your phone when you were here."

"I thought I could trust you!"

"Well, some people say I'm one of the good guys. But I need you to clear some things up."

"Things? What things?" Caroline asked.

"Things like the cops looking at me for Gina's death."

"What can I do about that?" Caroline's tone almost sounded as if she might laugh.

"I'm thinking, everything." Rick said. "I'm thinking we should talk. We need to come to a better arrangement than silence and suspicion."

Caroline paused and audibly took a breath. "I suppose if that goes on then, yes, it wouldn't be good for either of us. We can talk. This time. But you realize you cannot become part of my life."

"I'm not interested in your life," Rick sneered to himself. "I'm just trying to sift the crap from my own."

"Such eloquence."

"I'm on my way."

"Come to the Gemini—" Caroline began.

"No. The Golden Horizon. I know the place. We'll meet there." Rick hung up. Now he had another phone call to make.

Rick looked at the well-stocked bar of the empty Golden Horizon Club. "You're not even going to off me a drink?"

"No." Caroline said as she sat at one of the tables. "Cut to the chase is a phrase I've heard."

"Fine. I know you're the one who sent the cops video of me and Gina." Rick thought of the blonde PI, and played a long shot. "I even know the PI you've had following me. She good, not great. Tell her blonde hair sticks out."

"She's blonde now?" Caroline asked.

"Yep." *Pay dirt*, Rick thought.

"I guess she also cannot be trusted."

"A lot like you."

"No. I trust all who are loyal to me. I give them shelter. Some, I give me love." Caroline gave Rick with a knowing glance.

"A nice fringe benefit, I admit. But it doesn't make up for framing me." Rick stepped closer to the table.

"You realize, at the time I had no knowledge of—"

"You do now." Rick cut in. "And I need you to set things right."

Caroline paused. She smiled to herself. "Tell me why I should rid you of something that might benefit me?"

"Benefit you?" Rick asked and gripped his hips.

"Yes. It gives me a means to, well, to ask you to do certain things. If you do, the police will never gain *more* evidence of how you and Gina—"

"Bullshit! The only reason you don't want to help clear me is to save your own ass." Rick let a thought that had swirled in the back of his mind even when in bed with Caroline. He let it come forward as he shouted. "Admit it! You killed Gina!"

Caroline stiffened, but relaxed almost as quickly. She took a long, silent breath and looked straight at Rick. "You have no evidence."

Now Rick passed, and then let loose with another long shot. "Wrong! Why do you think I wanted to meet you and not just talk over the phone?"

"I don't see how—"

"I'm an investigator! And despite what you might think, I'm good. And you lady, you have one hell of a record going way beyond all of this." Rick threw his arms out and looked around the scarlet and golden trimmed club. "Prostitution pays for it. Your past is what will bring you down."

Caroline stood quickly and knocked her chair back. Her face contorted in emotions Rick could not judge as real or acted. "And would you enjoy seeing my fall? Did we mean nothing?"

"Okay. Maybe." Rick said in a low voice and stepped toward Caroline. "Then make it worth something. What I have I can hide. But I need to know all facts involved if I'm to make it all disappear."

Caroline looked off and became silent. Rick began to think his big ploy and all his recent effort was about to fail. He felt a pit opening beneath him. Then Caroline took a deep breath and spoke again.

"Gina betrayed me." She sat in the next chair and leaned on the table. "I could have given her all she desired. I wanted her to be with me. Me, not Genevieve."

"So you felt double betrayed." Rick walked over and picked up the fallen chair.

"Yes. I thought I could make Gina—that I could make her—" Caroline halted.

"Into another you."

"Yes. A sister, if you will."

"And a lover."

"Yes. Of course." Caroline glanced at Rick.

"So who told you Gina had screwed—sorry, betrayed you?"

"Gina herself," Caroline sighed. "And Genevieve—d'Angevin, although they did not know it at the time."

"Your spy was watching her?" Rick asked.

"No. I overheard them come to a bargain. Gina was wearing a micro-bud unit in her ear so I could guide her. It is discreet but old technology. Maybe that is why d'Angevin did notice the signal before she bit the device it from Gina's ear."

"Ouch."

"They did not realize the mic of her unit was still on when d'Angevin had made Gina an offer to spy on me. Gina accepted. Perhaps I would have as well, in her position. But I could not allow her to be a spy and reveal me to d'Avengin or her mercenaries. I could not even allow Gina to come back to the Golden Horizon."

"Did you know who you were setting her up with?"

Caroline went silent.

"Did you?" Rick pushed the question.

"Yes. I suspected d'Angevin had come here, as well. It is in her nature to micro-manage. I'm sure she is even the one who melted down the golden scepter and Alden's other treasures at her family villa."

"A real take-charge gal." Rick growled. "A brazen thief. But maybe not a killer."

Caroline turned and looked at Rick. "Are you so shocked? You are a killer yourself."

"I had to fight to live. It was self-defense."

"So was mine!" Caroline threw out her hands. "You did as I had to, as did I. No difference!"

"Big difference. I fought mercenaries, you killed a young woman."

"If I hadn't, she would have caused me to be killed. Would you want that? We can be lovers now! Do you want me to make love to you or die?"

Rick looked down. He saw Caroline's refection as she starred at him. He looked at her. "I don't think Gina had to die."

"Then you are wrong! I intercepted her, and yes, I killed her. And I am alive now because I did!"

"No. You killed her because you were betrayed. It was one part calculation and one part rage. Your old lover had flipped the girl you wanted. You hated that. You hated being betrayed by Gina. And by d'Avengin, again."

"Of course!" Caroline shrieked and appeared to lose control. She tensed as if to jump at Rick. Then she sat back in a bizarre, swift return to normal. Caroline smiled. "But we can still be together. We are very much the same—"

Caroline halted. Her eyes fell to the left as she searched her mind.

"Go ahead," Rick said. "Say my name."

"Malik. Fredricks. Maybe you like Freddy? No?"

"No. We may have knocked boots, but we are not the same." Rick stepped back and glanced to the hidden entrance.

"What does this mean? If we are not together, then get out! I don't want to see you! Seline!" Caroline cried out but no one came.

"She's already been picked up." Rick nodded at a memory.

"Picked up?"

"Yeah. She was here when the police techies came in—" Rick looked straight at Caroline "—and wired the place."

"What do you—?" Caroline realized what Rick meant just as she began her question. It would be the last words she spoke to him.

The hidden door opened from the outside. Hardin, Whilton, and two female officers came in. Other officers stood in the hall passed the closet and the two mannequins still naked and still smiling.

Caroline stared off with a face of rage as the police took her arms and cuffed her. She made eye contact with no one as if looking out to a distant horizon she would never reach.

Later in the night, Rick returned home. There was beer. There was Bushmills. Rick just enjoyed the darkness. At least it was not at the bottom of a pit. And tomorrow, he could leave his home, and no one would care. Especially not the police.

In the morning, Rick sat at his desk and powered up his laptop. Maybe he would do some searches that would give him info to better his life. Maybe he would play solitaire. He was sure his laptop had solitaire, somewhere. Maybe even spider solitaire, although he had seen enough of those spinners and other forms of webs, lately. He sat and stared at his browser's screen. Suddenly someone stared back at him.

Genevieve Elle d'Angevin smiled at Rick. He was getting used to looking at attractive women, some with knowing smiles. This one looked as though she already had her hand inside Rick's shorts and held his own family jewels in her long, red fingernails.

Rick stayed focused on d'Angevin. He thought of two things to ignore so he didn't tip off d'Avengin to their presence. Thankfully, they were out of camera shot. One was stuck inside the middle drawer of the desk he bought at an estate sale of a former client. The drawer was still overstuffed with junk mail and other useless paper from the previous owner.

The other thing was behind him in a pot. The plant it held was dead. The camera hidden by the dried leaves was live. d'Avengin felt certain her connection was secure and adequately scrambled, but the camera wasn't tied to Wi-Fi or any internet connection. Its video resolution could be better, but it had a great mic and d'Avengin spoke very clearly. He couldn't record on his laptop, but he could still record their conversation.

"Mr. Fredricks, nice to meet the thorn in my side." d'Angevin said.

"People say it other ways, but, yeah, I get that a lot." Rick grumbled.

"Did you ever get milk?" d'Angevin asked and her smile widened.

Rick cocked his eyebrows.

"Your refrigerator has an app." d'Avengin continued. "It's supposed to send a list to your phone. It activated it for you.

Rick narrowed his state. He knew d'Avengin was showing off her hacking prowess. He had to admit that, yes, she was a bitch. And probably a tough opponent in the mental boxing ring. Rick felt he should adjust his mouthpiece.

"I never knew it." Rick lied. He did know. He never switched on the sensor because he hated the idea of a machine sending a message out to any hacker, or worse, about how much beer he drank.

"Not to sound offensive, but there is a great deal you don't understand." d'Avengin said with smile as she slashed him verbally.

"Maybe. Like why you're making direct contact." Rick said, then jabbed. "All your goons dead?"

"As a matter of fact—well, let's skip unpleasantries." d'Angevin looked off and shook her head, slightly. "But I do have openings in my, let's call it an organization. You have proven yourself resourceful, or at least that you possess an inherent skill for survival. I can use such skill."

"I'll bet." Rick saw an opportunity to jab d'Avengin, again. Maybe if she was pissed she might shout out something incriminating. "What the hell were you thinking?"

"Can you be—"

"More specific?" Rick cut in. "Sure. Why screw yourself over. You had a good life. Now, it's shot to hell."

"Dear, man, I said there was a lot you don't understand, that you don't know. I can—"

Rick cut in again. "Maybe, but this isn't physics. I wonder why a person who had a rich life took a turn that ended up sharing a low-rent hidey-hole with a bunch of mercenaries."

"One never knows what the fates weave, Mr. Fredricks. I assume you imagined a better fate than you enjoy."

"I wasn't a born lotto winner. You were. But I guess even that was chump change compared to the money coming into Alden. Was it seeing other people's bank accounts get stacked while you were cut out? Kept a figurehead with an empty wallet?"

d'Angevin's smile relaxed, but she didn't frown. But Rick took it that his angle was getting past her defenses.

"I assure you, my own accounts were never empty." d'Angevin said.

"But you still wanted some of that fat cash you saw others enjoying. Others who weren't royal, or even classy. Too you."

d'Angevin sighed. "Such a typical, proletarian perspective."

"You act like an ace hacker, but you didn't pull off some electronic heist. You just robbed the store old style. You stole the crown jewels and hawked them."

"There was slightly more sophistication than that." d'Angevin's voice almost lowered to a growl.

"Not much." Rick shrugged.

"We just went through a pandemic," d'Angevin took a breath collected herself. "A lot of people, the rich included, have yet to recover."

"Judging from the suit I can see and the earrings, looks like you recovered just fine. So why dig a deeper hole? For all your wealth, stolen and otherwise, you're on the run." Rick leaned toward the screen.

"If I am on the run, then it's only over-worked and under-staffed law enforcement that's chasing me. I like my odds of freedom. Yours, though? Dear man, you must understand that your position is not so fortunate."

Rick realized the news of Caroline's bust had not yet leaked. He didn't inform d'Angevin but strung her along.

"But fortune could be yours," d'Angevin continued. "All you need to do is swear an oath to me, now. And then get on a plane."

"You make it sound like I'm getting knighted." Rick said.

"Knighthood is honorary. The benefits I offer are more practical. Not the least of which is your continued health. A better future." d'Angevin cocked her head and stared as if aiming a through a sniper scope. "Your life."

Rick shrugged and stopped himself from glancing back at the camera in the pot. "So, my life is on the line?"

"Of course, dear man. Of course."

"Well, then how can I refuse?" Rick shrugged.

"Then you agree?"

Rick lowered his head in his best act of looking resigned. "No choice."

"Indeed." d'Angevin smiled again. "You will receive an email. Old fashioned, yes, but secure. Be seeing you, Mr.

Fredricks. And please use the forthcoming allowance to at least buy a tie before we meet."

"Right. One with Alden's family seal."

"They come in silk. Good bye!" d'Angevin vanished.

Rick thought that, ultimately, he didn't have much of a choice. His act of bowing to d'Angevin was ducking a punch. If d'Angevin had skipped the US, he might actually get a nice plane ride. And maybe some cash in his shrunken bank account. But he knew that soon after that he would get steal or lead through his skull or spine. Likely both. Maybe he still would. But not before he counterpunched.

Rick closed his laptop. He glanced at the hidden camera and smiled. Then he rolled out the overstuffed desk drawer. He finished in it and pulled out the large emerald and gold ring. He had pocketed it from Caroline's loot that she obviously stole from d'Angevin. And so that stolen wealth kept spreading. But it might have better uses than just for cash. He tried to put the ring on his middle finger. Its band was too narrow.

"Damn. I really wanted to flip her off in style."

Rick reached over and picked up his phone. He hit a number that he usually associated with dread. There were several rings before an exasperated voice answered.

"Hello? What?"

"Yo, Hardin. Nice to hear your voice. How's life?"

"Wait, Fredricks? Again? Fuck off! What do you want anyway?"

"Those Interpol agents, they still in town?"

"Yeah—wait! How do you know—?"

"Tell them to give me a call." Rick said and rolled the emerald ring in his fingers. "Tell them they really want to talk to me. And keep Caroline Krymménos nice and safe. They'll want to talk to her, too."

"Why?"

"Because, detective boner, I'm about to punch a hole in the world. And you can either hold onto the edge, or fall in."

END